THE MEDICINE MEN

JOHN LLOYD FRASER

A Guide to Natural Medicine

THAMES / METHUEN

First published in Great Britain 1981
by Eyre Methuen Ltd with Methuen Paperbacks Ltd
11 New Fetter Lane, London EC4P 4EE
in association with
Thames Television International Ltd
149 Tottenham Court Road, London W1P 91L

Printed in Great Britain
by Richard Clay (The Chaucer Press) Ltd
Bungay, Suffolk

ISBN 0 423 00190 6 (Hardcover edition)
ISBN 0 423 00180 9 (Paperback edition)

Contents

Picture Acknowledgments

The illustrations are reproduced by courtesy of the following organisations and individuals:

8, 12, 13, 14: Wellcome Trustees; *18*: Chelsea Physic Garden; *20(l)*: Alan Howard, Anglia TV; *20(r)*: Philip King, Anglia TV; *21*: Alan Howard, Anglia TV; *24, 25*: Mary Evans Picture Library; *27*: Chelsea Physic Garden; *29(l)*: Osterreichische Nationalbibliothek; *29(r)*: Bob Hobbs, Anglia TV; *31*: Nicolette Hallett, Anglia TV; *34(tl & r)*: Natural Light Pictures; *34(bl & r)*: Allen Paterson; *37, 38, 39*: Chelsea Physic Garden; *40, 42, 45*: Natural Light Pictures; *47*: Philip King, Anglia TV; *51(l)* Allen Paterson; *51(r), 52, 53*: Natural Light Pictures; *57*: Philip King, Anglia TV; *64*: Wellcome Trustees; *66*: Oxford Orthopaedic Engineering Centre; *68*: British Chiropractors Association; *69*: Kirksville College of Osteopathic Medicine, Missouri; *71*: Palmer College of Chiropractic, Davenport, Iowa; *72, 75, 79*: Bob Hobbs, Anglia TV; *81*: Alan Howard, Anglia TV; *84, 85*: Nick Bartlett/Back Pain Association; *87*: Wellcome Trustees; *88, 90*: Mary Evans Picture Library; *92*: Philip King, Anglia TV; *95(l)*: Mary Evans Picture Library; *95(r)*: Bob Hobbs, Anglia TV; *96*: Philip King, Anglia TV; *97*: Natural Light Pictures; *103, 104*: Philip King, Anglia TV; *110*: Mary Evans Picture Library; *112(l)*: Wellcome Trustees; *112(r)*: Philip King, Anglia TV; *115*: Psychic Press; *117*: Bob Hobbs, Anglia TV; *119*: Harry Oldfield; *121*: Iain Coates, Anglia TV; *125*: Philip King, Anglia TV; *126*: Phil Edwardes; *127*: Philip King, Anglia TV; *128, 131(l)*: Will Hazell; *131(r)*: Jean-Loup Charmet/Bibliotheque Nationale, Paris; *132*: Roger Keen, Anglia TV; *133*: Bob Hobbs, Anglia TV; *134*: Anglia TV; *135*: Natural Light Pictures; *136*: Anglia TV; *137*: Natural Light Pictures; *139*: Will Hazell; *141*: John Sherley-Dale; *144*: Nicolette Hallett, Anglia TV; *148*: Anglo–Chinese Educational Institute; *150*: George Lewith; *151*: Julian Kenyon; *153*: Anglia TV/Julian Kenyon; *157(tl & r)*: Bob Hobbs, Anglia TV/Science Museum/Wellcome Trustees; *157(bl & r)*: Nicolette Hallett, Anglia TV; *158*: George Lewith; *159, 161*: James Ravilious; *162*: Julian Kenyon; *165*: Natural Light Pictures; *172*: Deutscher Bäderverband; *174*: Wellcome Trustees; *176, 177, 178*: Health Education Council; *179*: Anglia TV; *183*: Nicolette Hallett, Anglia TV; *187*: Mary Evans Picture Library; *187(inset)*: Deutscher Bäderverband; *189*: Goethe Institute; *190*: Newman Turner Publications; *194*: Punch; *196*: D. R. Cleevely.

Acknowledgements

The preparation of this book, and the series of television films with which it is associated, was carried out in close collaboration with my friend and indefatigable colleague, Garfield Kennedy.

I enjoyed several conversations with Brian Inglis whose advice was invaluable.

My thanks are also due to the many medicine men and women who gave of their time and shared their knowledge and experience.

The staff of the Anglia Television Stills Department invariably produced work of a high standard and were equal to any request.

I want to thank all the film crews who contributed to the making of the *The Medicine Men* during 1980–81. I had the good fortune to work with a gifted film editor, Gil Edgeley.

Finally, I want to thank my wife and children for so generously tolerating my preoccupation.

The author and publisher gratefully acknowledge Herbert Benson and Collins Publishers for permission to reproduce 'The Relaxation Response' on pp. 108—109. The recipe for the 'Grant Loaf' on p. 192 is reprinted by permission of Faber and Faber Ltd from Your Daily Food: Recipe for Survival *by Doris Grant.*

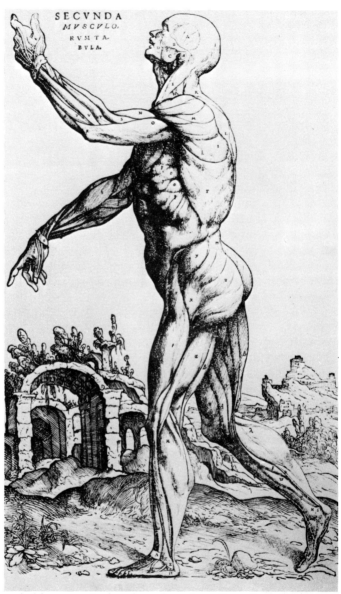

Remarkably accurate drawings, based on dissection of the human body, marked the beginning of the quest for a scientific understanding of how our bodies function. This woodcut was published in 1543.

Introduction

One of the first duties of the physician is to educate people not
to take medicine.

Sir William Osler

When primitive man became ill he turned to the medicine man.
In some parts of the world today the sick first consult the
medicine man. In the advanced countries we are increasingly
seeking help from alternative medical practitioners – our
equivalent of the medicine men.

Not so very long ago doctors could anticipate a run of
inquiries about acupuncture or osteopathy from their patients
in the wake of newspaper articles or a television programme.
All practitioners of alternative medicine were regarded as
'quacks'. A few dismissive phrases, coupled with a stern warning about the dangers of relying on medically unqualified
people, would have been sufficient to dissuade all but the most
determined. But now things have changed. Some doctors
openly admit that they refer patients to alternative practitioners, particularly osteopaths, and are themselves treated when
necessary.

Doctors, having been primed with six or more years of
scientific education, find it difficult to judge the merits of
alternative therapies with any degree of objectivity. If you go to
a typical doctor and ask him to refer you to an acupuncturist or
a hypnotist, he will more than likely refuse; he does not see it as
his business to act as agent for people he would regard as
'quacks'. To such a doctor there can be no marriage between
his methods and whatever he thinks the acupuncturist or hypnotist does. He has been conditioned by his training to reject
such an association as unethical.

Until recently, doctors could have been disciplined for sending patients to alternative practitioners. They may do so now

provided that they maintain control of the patient's treatment, a condition that, in practice, is little observed.

It seems that what people want is to be able to consult an alternative medical practitioner as they might attend a dentist for their teeth. But they want to do so with the approval of their doctors. They do not want to feel uncomfortable when they admit that they have been to see an osteopath or an acupuncturist.

Too many people are turning to alternative medicine for it all to be ignored or dismissed as quackery. In rejecting the claims of alternative medicine for so long doctors presumably thought that they were acting in the best interests of their patients. But the determination with which alternative medicine has been repelled suggests defensiveness.

If a patient is helped towards recovery through the ministrations of a chiropractor, after he has tried conventional treatment without success, it does mean that orthodox medicine has failed. Surely there is only one response to such a case: welcome the patient's recovery and acknowledge its source. It would be unfair to suggest that most doctors would not take this view, but there are some who certainly would not. To the layman, the medical profession gives every impression of being unduly concerned with maintaining its monopoly. It does not want to be seen to fail where an alternative therapy seems to work. But what has happened to make many of us doubt the effectiveness of orthodox medicine?

The person who has recovered from serious illness after surgery and skilled after-care can only be thankful that he is once again fit and well. This is an everyday occurrence in hospitals up and down the country. This is modern medicine at its best, the kind that has earned for its practitioners, particularly at the surgical level, the reputations of supermen. The patient is happy, his relatives are thankful and full of praise for the skill of the doctors who attended him. Where is the dissatisfaction here?

The medical profession would earn rather less plaudits from a person who following back or hip surgery is left with stiffness or pain. True, the severe pre-operative pain has gone, but it has been replaced with a condition that will probably last a lifetime. No blame can attach to the surgeon for backing his judgement

10

that an operation was necessary; neither can the patient be criticised for consenting to an operation because 'doctor knows best'.

Comparatively few people have to submit to major surgery, but thousands of people are kept 'ticking over' with the help of synthetic chemical drugs. They have regained their health as a result of drug therapy, but they often do not feel quite themselves. The heart may be beating more regularly, the lungs are freer than they used to be, the blood pressure is down, but at the same time the patient may have contracted severe headaches, nausea, or pains or discomfort in another part of the body. In other words he has joined the army of people who suffer side-effects from many modern medicines. Often the side-effects are so severe that the patient decides that the condition which he presented to the doctor is preferable to the effects caused by the prescribed drug.

It is from this group that alternative medical practitioners draw many of their patients. They are determined to recover their health, but they cannot and will not accept that being bombarded by powerful chemical drugs is the right way to do it. They are seeking effective treatment, but they want it to be gentler because they instinctively recognise that long-lasting recovery of health is unlikely to result from a 'course' of powerful drugs. It is probably untypical, but the frequent response of one doctor when faced with yet another drug company's salesman, laden with glossy literature and free samples, is, 'If it's still in use in a year's time, I might consider using it.'

People who have exhausted what orthodox medicine can offer are often told by their doctors that they 'will have to live with' their particular complaint. They have to accept that orthodox medicine can do no more. They turn to alternative medicine in desperation as a 'last resort'. Others only reluctantly leave orthodox medicine for the largely uncharted waters of alternative medicine because there is something lacking in the treatment. It is probably true to say that most patients of alternative medical practitioners have in common a dissatisfaction with orthodox medicine. Doctors would say that often too much is expected of them.

Most patients can no doubt be dealt with effectively in a few

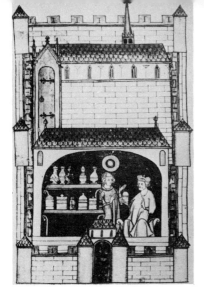

A thirteenth century apothecary and his assistant in a castle pharmacy.

minutes, but many require more than the average six minutes that general practitioners spend with each of their patients.

Some patients want nothing more than to talk about themselves and their troubles with someone who appears to be, and very often is, a caring individual. They feel cheated, angry, and embarrassed if they are cut short and handed a piece of paper to take to the chemist. From such treatment alternative medical practitioners reap the benefit because they, above all, give their patients what most of them need, and that is time. Doctors, for their part, say that they are trained as medical attendants; they should not be expected to act as counsellors, social workers, clergymen, psychiatrists or proxy aunts and uncles to the patients on their 'panel'. In country areas the doctor is still a 'figure' in the community, but in urban areas patients are increasingly coming to realise that they are the fodder for a vast bureaucratic machine which processes illness. They are numbers on a card or computer. Regardless of their complaint, patients want to be recognised as individual people with problems and preoccupations uniquely different from every other person.

Whole Body Medicine

The application of time to diagnosis and treatment is indivisible from the alternative medical approach to health which is variously named 'whole', 'holistic', or 'total' medicine. In dealing with illness most alternative practitioners see themselves as treating a body that is sick or malfunctioning. They do not regard the body as a piece of machinery, parts of which need repair. A doctor presented with a liver problem may feel his work is done if he treats the liver. A typical alternative practitioner would want to know why the liver in that particular body became sick. He may or may not have the ability to find out, but he will nevertheless treat the body and its illness as a whole with the intention of encouraging the body to heal itself. Alternative medical practitioners often claim that the orthodox profession ignores the demonstrated capacity of the body to heal itself. Orthodox doctors argue that while this might be all very well for trivial or psychosomatic illnesses, it would represent a serious dereliction of their duty to rely on this approach

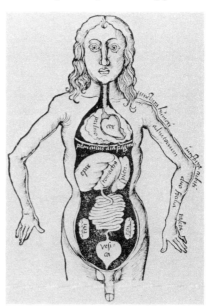

This early sixteenth-century woodcut illustrates what little understanding man had of his own anatomy.

for serious illness. But what do alternative medical practitioners mean when they talk of treating the whole body?

The idea that the body is not simply physical, but is made up of the mind and the spirit interrelating with it, is of ancient origin. It has been a running theme throughout the history of

13

medicine; present in the thinking of physicians as an ideal, but one that was never widely adopted. The practice of conventional medicine was found to be more conveniently managed if the body was treated as a collection of parts rather than an indivisible whole. Alternative medicine is now the guardian of an approach to health that claims that no part of the body can be made better unless the underlying cause is also discovered and treated.

It is a fundamental belief in alternative medicine that much trivial illness arises from the way we live our lives, a view shared by an increasing number of doctors. It's now generally recognised that food, environment, and our psychological state is of vital importance in maintaining health. Eating excessive amounts of animal fats, white flour, sugar, synthetic food, taking little or no exercise or recreation, overworking, bereavement, and unemployment are often responsible, more so than specific infections, for many trivial and some serious complaints. Doctors would not disagree with this – some actively promote this point of view – but would argue that

The comparatively recent innovation of crude antiseptic conditions in an operation of 1882. Carbolic acid is automatically spraying over the open wound.

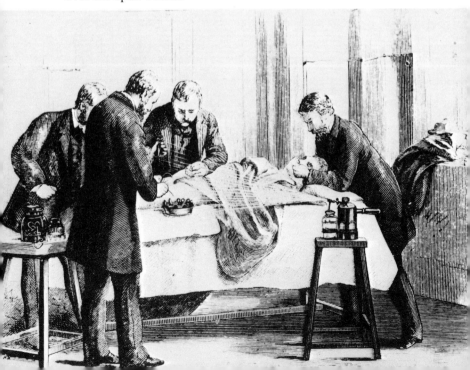

alternative medicine is often not effective against stress-related complaints which are common all over the developed world.

It is perhaps not surprising that doctors generally are critical or suspicious of alternative medical therapies. It's been estimated that at least one hundred and fifty different treatments qualify for the description 'alternative medicine'. Comparatively few are widely practised. Of those that are, only a few are generally agreed to be likely to achieve widespread recognition as effective therapies.

HERBALISM hardly qualifies as an 'alternative' because within living memory it was the ruling medical orthodoxy of the day. Some herbalists look forward to a time when we will once again go out into the fields and pick the herbs and plants that we need to rid us of sickness. This seems improbable, but it does seem possible that the many thousands of plants which have yet to be investigated scientifically might be the source of potentially valuable drugs. Before dismissing herbalism as an archaic medical method we should remember that digitalis or the foxglove is still a medical drug, and it was not so long ago that the Mexican yam was found to be the source of the active constituent of the contraceptive pill.

HOMOEOPATHY, deriving from the notion that 'likes can be cured by likes', has an uncertain future. It is relatively healthy in this country, but in America it has declined from the beginning of this century when there were about seventy homoeopathic hospitals and around ten thousand practitioners; now there are no homoeopathic hospitals and comparatively few homoeopaths. But homoeopathy thrives in India where there are said to be 300,000 homoeopathic practitioners and over fifty journals devoted to the subject.

OSTEOPATHY and **CHIROPRACTIC** are manipulative therapies whose future might best be assured by settling their largely historical differences and renaming themselves 'manipulators'. To the patient there is very little apparent difference between the two techniques although chiropractors readily admit that theirs is the more violent. It is interesting that doctors find themselves most at home with osteopathy and chiropractic, the most mechanistic of the alternative therapies.

HYPNOSIS has established a niche within the orthodox medical profession and is one of the few 'alternative' treatments available through the National Health Service. It is used for a number of complaints which formerly might have been treated with tranquillisers. Its most serious drawback is that it is a time-consuming technique.

If patients are worried, mistakenly, that their minds are going to be taken over during hypnosis they fear, again incorrectly, that **healing** is available only to those with religious belief. Of all the alternative therapies healers make the least demands on their patients. Most established healers have well-appointed consulting rooms from which they offer a service used by several thousand people every year.

Most people who find themselves drawn to alternative medicine find **radionics** hard to swallow. Radionics is a system of treating illness through the use of dowsing, the technique used by water-diviners. By a combination of dowsing and extrasensory perception practitioners claim to be able to diagnose the cause of a patient's illness. They can also treat at a distance. Radionics has to be taken on trust, but anyone who accepts water-divining will have little difficulty in grasping its essentials.

In the last five years, **acupuncture** has become respectable enough to be mentioned approvingly in medical journals. It is practised in several hospitals and by an increasing number of doctors. Acupuncturists in Britain and elsewhere seem to be dividing into two camps: traditional and modern. The traditional school believes that it is only possible to practise acupuncture after the ancient system of points and meridians has been fully mastered. The modernists claim that needles inserted in the general area of the acupuncture point for a particular ailment will be as effective as the accurate needling demanded of a traditionally-trained practitioner. Traditionalists claim that the hit-or-miss technique of some acupuncturists is a travesty of the elegance of the Chinese system which has been practised for some five thousand years.

Naturopathy as a therapy relies on the body's ability to heal itself naturally. It cannot do this unless its need for good food and adequate rest and exercise, allied to a psychologically buoyant attitude to life, is fulfilled. Naturopaths claim that of all natural therapies their approach, if generally adopted, could effect a considerable improvement in health.

16

This book does not pretend to be an exhaustive account of natural or alternative medicine in Britain. It is essentially intended as a guide to anyone interested in knowing more about the leading natural therapies or wanting some knowledge about what to expect prior to a consultation with a practitioner. Each chapter, and the reference section, gives information about how to contact either a practitioner or the representative organisation, if there is one. Like other callings, natural medicine has its incompetents and charlatans, but they can be avoided if you rely on a knowledgeable recommendation, or the practitioner of your choice is known and approved of by the representative body.

Nicholas Culpeper (1616–1654), compiler of the best known British herbal.

Herbalism

Nature to repair, draws physics from the fields . . .

John Dryden

The alarm clock rings. You stagger to the kitchen and make an infusion of the leaves of the plant *Camellia sinensis* – in other words, a cup of tea, one of the world's most popular plant stimulants. If you have coffee for breakfast you are again taking a plant remedy – for heart disease, dropsy and migraine – although it's hard to believe that instant coffee ever had anything to do with the plant *Coffea arabica*. If you have an apple you are dosing yourself with a plant remedy which over the centuries has been prescribed for intestinal complaints, rheumatism, bronchial, gastric, and kidney conditions, and anaemia. Your main meal can hardly fail to contain an ancient medicine. Lettuce, radish, leek, onion and potatoes all have therapeutic properties; carrots are known to increase the number of red blood corpuscles. Cabbage is still prescribed for disturbances of the alimentary canal although few would wish to follow Plato's recommendation of half a cabbage daily.

Herbalism is more widely practised than any other fringe or alternative medicine. Far more people throughout the world depend upon herbs and plants for their medicine than use chemical drugs. The herbalist is a respected figure throughout much of Africa, India and Latin America. The Chinese, who have relied on herbal remedies for centuries, are attempting to marry Western scientific health care with their thriving system of traditional medicine based upon a combination of herbalism and acupuncture, much of it provided by 'bare-foot doctors'. The World Health Organisation is actively promoting herbal medicine and other relevant alternative systems throughout the Third World.

The poorer countries are of necessity having to consider ways

(a) Pharmacists in the early part of this century stocked mostly herbal medicines.
(b) Today a complex range of chemical preparations has replaced herbal remedies.

of making their traditional systems of medicine workable, but in Western countries there is a discernible retreat from technological medicine accompanied by a marked interest in herbal and other unorthodox medical therapies.

There is little possibility that doctors will again start prescribing opium for insomnia or rhubarb for intestinal problems, but what seems to be happening in Britain is that herbalism has gone 'underground': we have become a nation of self-prescribers. Health stores, now perhaps the equivalent of the pharmacist who, in the early part of this century, would prescribe for trivial complaints, say that their customers tend to be people who, as far as possible, want to be responsible for their own health: they are not opposed to orthodox medicine for serious illness, but they believe that herbal medicine (and 'natural' food) can help with trivial complaints.

One shop that serves almost as a barometer to assess the state of herbal medicine in Britain is Baldwin's, probably London's oldest surviving herbalist. Around the walls are jars and bottles of dried herbs and herbal tinctures; behind the counter are ranks of drawers marked with Latin names of medicinal herbs. It would be an unusual day for Baldwin's not to be continually busy from early in the morning to closing time, advising and prescribing about health matters and supplying herbal remedies for specific ailments. Many customers come in for a pint or a half of sarsaparilla, a refreshing non-alcoholic herbal drink which is also said to be a tonic. Whatever it does must be effective because Baldwin's has a regular army of sarsaparilla

An English pharmacy of the 1920s. Most treatments were still of herbal origin although some chemically-based preparations were available.

drinkers from the surrounding area. Most customers come with a minor medical problem. A singer explains that she is starting a new engagement, but has developed a sore throat. Because chemical drugs upset her, she wants to try a herbal remedy. She receives a sympathetic hearing from the herbalist who prescribes, at a cost of a few pence, a twist of paper containing Red Sage. The preparation and dosage is carefully explained; the medicine may or may not work, but the 'patient' thinks it will, an important factor in any medical treatment.

It is startling to realise that many of the herbs or plants prescribed by a modern herbalist would also have been used by the ancient medicine man in practice centuries ago.

21

The Earliest Medicine Men

From the earliest time man grew both his food and his medicine. Often a plant or herb had a dual role: it served as food, and also had a therapeutic effect. The globe artichoke, for example, now consumed only as a vegetable, was once the recognised treatment for a poisoned liver. Over many hundreds of years man carried out what has been called 'the longest clinical trial in history'. He found plants and herbs and ate them. Some satisfied his hunger or cured his ailments, but many others must have made him ill or even killed him. Gradually he learned which herbs and plants could be eaten for food, which were efficacious in curing illnesses, and which were dangerous. Prehistoric man would have handed on information about medicinal plants by word of mouth, but eventually written language enabled his successors to compile accounts of herbs and plants and their medicinal use.

The earliest known herbal appeared in China in about 3000 BC, the work of the Emperor Shen Nung. Modern herbalists frequently cite this first herbal in support of their claim that we have only scratched the surface of medical herbalism. Shen Nung's herbal contained an entry for a plant called *ma-huang* which was said to be helpful for lung and bronchial complaints; it also could control fever and improve circulation. Not until the late nineteenth century, however, was *ma-huang* identified as ephedra, and not until the early years of this century was ephedra used as the basis for the manufacture of ephedrine, the first 'modern' medicine to bring effective relief to asthmatics. We can only guess at what remains to be discovered in the 300,000 known plants that are found on earth, only a small proportion of which have been evaluated.

Herbal medicine was also practised in India and Egypt where it was allied to a belief in gods or spirits and magic. In Mesopotamia, the Sumerians compiled their first herbal a few hundred years after the Chinese in about 2,500 BC. They seem to have had a well-established system of herbal medicine relying on many plants which are still in therapeutic use today – belladonna, opium, liquorice, garlic, henbane, saffron, thyme, and cannabis. The theory and practice of herbalism was not comprehensively codified until the civilisation of Ancient

Greece; it produced several men who not only acknowledged the medical importance of herbs, but also in their differing ways laid the foundations of a medical philosophy which finds more than an echo in the practice of modern medicine.

Hippocrates, known as the Father of Medicine, believed in the natural power of the body to heal itself – the *vis medicatrix naturae* – but he also recognised the efficacy of herbs and plants and recommended their use in many illnesses. Doctors today no longer formally swear the Hippocratic Oath – which in essence reminded doctors that their purpose was to care efficiently for the sick – but most would have no difficulty in agreeing that they follow its precepts. Although Hippocrates approved of the use of herbs and plants, he did not compile a herbal. Aristotle wrote about herbs and plants more as a botanist than as a herbalist. His writings inspired his contemporary, Theophrastus, to develop them into two works describing the growth and uses of plants; they were to remain influential botanical texts for many centuries.

By the first century AD, Greek and other accounts of plants and herbs needed collating and the man who took on this considerable task was a physician named Dioscorides. Being an army doctor, he travelled extensively in Europe where he studied and collected material for his great work, *De Materia Medica.* As a result, Dioscorides became the undisputed authority on plants and medicine until about the 15th or 16th century.

The influence of the Greeks in medicine and botany was led for many centuries by Galen whom many regard as second only to Hippocrates. Galen, like Hippocrates, was a physician, but he approached illness from a different standpoint. Curiously, Hippocrates' belief in the power of the body to heal itself is more in tune with the alternative medicines of today, whereas Galen believed that medicines – derived from plants, animals and minerals – were necessary to vanquish disease. His influence, like that of Theophrastus, Dioscorides and other Greek writers and physicians, survived the Dark Ages. Medical teaching for several centuries was based on the ideas of Galen, but from about the 15th century the uncomplicated approach of the Greeks to the medicinal use of herbs and plants again became dominant but was overlaid with magic, superstition, and

23

(a) Dioscorides (first century AD)
(b) Galen (*c.* 130–202 AD)

religion. It gave rise in the 16th century to a view of plants and
herbs which the Greeks might well have found untenable. The
most powerful of these 'new' ideas was the Doctrine of Signatures.

The Doctrine of Signatures

The Doctrine of Signatures appealed to the mediaeval mind
because it had a superficial logic and, in an age almost obsessed
with finding out about the meaning of the physical world, it was
seen as evidence that a grand design existed. It was thought
that the Creator had not acted haphazardly in making the
plant world. Paracelsus (1493–1541), an Austrian physician,
developed the doctrine which proposed that all medicinal
24

Paracelsus (1493–1541)

plants had a purpose to cure a disease or regenerate an organ that could be related to its shape. Thus, a heart-shaped plant was intended for heart complaints; the walnut and the nutmeg were thought to be medicines for brain disorders. The shape of the plant was its 'signature' and curiously, as a practical theory of medicine, it sometimes seemed to work. However, it was eventually seen to be untenable when it was realised that many plants were medically efficacious but lacked a signature. As a result, the Doctrine of Signatures declined and was discarded around the middle of the seventeenth century at a time when the production of herbals, encouraged by the invention of printing, had reached its height.

Probably the best known British herbal is that of Nicholas Culpeper who in 1652 produced an 'everybody's guide to herbalism'. Culpeper was regarded as an opportunist populariser by scholars for rendering into English texts which previously had been available only in Latin. He was also criticised for spreading the Doctrine of Signatures when it had already been discredited and for attempting to marry herbalism, increasingly being seen as a scientific study, with astrology. Culpeper,

25

however, was fulfilling a need and his book sold widely, and is still in print today.

Until the 17th century nearly all medicines were derived from plants. They were dispensed by physicians, apothecaries, local or wandering herbalists, and by individuals for themselves and their families. Informally dispensed folk medicine was the recognised method for ordinary people to cope with illness, and this remained true until the early twentieth century. However, herbal medicine as practised by physicians began moving towards chemical and mineral constituents from about the middle of the seventeenth century. Partially influenced by the teaching of Paracelsus, apothecaries began supplying minerals and metals as therapeutic medicines; sulfur, iron, arsenic, and mercury were effective in a blunderbuss kind of way for a variety of illnesses often caused by over-indulgence rather than natural causes.

For much of the nineteenth century the fight against disease was carried on in a climate of ignorance of the need for sanitation and little was known of the way the body contracted or repelled invading organisms. While scientific and medical research sought a 'magic bullet' in the form of metals, minerals, or chemicals, or a combination of all three, to combat diseases, herbal medicine continued to flourish. There was, at the same time, an undertow of dissatisfaction with plant medicine because it was clearly powerless against many serious diseases. Chemical medicine seemed to have potential. The race to develop it was, for most of the nineteenth century, a metropolitan preoccupation of doctors and scientists, and later embryo industrialists who could see the commercial possibilities in large-scale manufacture of popular and effective medicines.

Now that we have become used to chemical drugs it is easy to forget that pill-based medicine only began in the early years of this century. Dr Donald Vaughan, who is 83, remembers that when he began in general practice in Norfolk in the 1920's most of the medicines he used were derived from herbs and plants; the British Pharmacopaeia then was predominantly an account of remedies derived from plant or natural sources. Some of them were prescribed as pills or tablets, but they contained an active ingredient that had once been in a growing plant. Dr Vaughan's Gladstone bag contained remedies such as rhubarb

26

Frontispiece to Parkinson's Herbal published in 1640.

for digestive problems, belladonna for fever, and opium as a sedative or for pain. *Digitalis* (Foxglove) was a heart stimulant without equal and continues to be widely prescribed today, but strychnine and aconite were also used for cardiac complaints.

Dr Vaughan, who still practises medicine, says that patients' common complaints have changed very little during this century. 'In my early days in practice they always seemed to have something wrong with their insides. There were plenty of medicines around to stir them up. Now patients seem to be under a lot of stress and strain and they want sleeping pills and tranquillisers. Sleeping tablets as such hardly existed when I began in practice.' Dr Vaughan believes that we should not regard today's immensely effective drugs as props to help us cope with life. 'What I would like to see is doctors educated in minimum prescribing, and for patients to accept that not all ills need pills.'

Modern Herbal Medicine

If you decide that you want to consult a herbalist you may experience difficulty in finding one. In larger cities you may find entries in the *Yellow Pages*, or you could contact the National Institute of Medical Herbalists whose address is in the reference section. Because herbs and plants can be powerful medicines and in careless or untrained hands could be dangerous, it's a sensible precaution to find out if the practitioner of your choice is a member of the National Institute of Medical Herbalists. A member of the NIMH will normally have undergone a part-time or full-time course lasting four years covering not only pure herbalism – the study of the structure of plants and their medical application – but also anatomy and physiology, and the pathology of disease. The National Institute of Medical Herbalists does not claim that their courses provide the equivalent of a medical degree; they believe that they provide a thorough training which serves as a safeguard for both practitioner and patient.

John Hyde of Leicester runs one of the leading herbal clinics in the country. Hyde's Clinic could be mistaken for a general

(a) An apothecary and his apprentice (1500). Herbal wisdom was handed down through generations of apothecaries who both diagnosed ailments and prescribed treatments.
(b) Future herbal practitioners are instructed by tutor, Hein Zelystra (centre) of the National Institute of Medical Herbalists.

practitioner's surgery. It has an appointments system (although you might have to wait several weeks), a sparsely furnished waiting room with a pile of aging magazines, and consulting rooms which contain much of the hardware of orthodox medicine. John Hyde conveys the friendly confidence of a family physician. Inevitably, some patients address him as 'doctor', but he discourages this because he is content to be known as a 'herbal practitioner'. He sees patients from all parts of the country and from all walks of life suffering from all kinds of complaints. Like many practitioners in alternative medicine, John Hyde derives considerable satisfaction in numbering among his patients several doctors and nurses.

29

Most patients come to him as a last resort. They are prepared to try anything, and that includes herbalism which, John Hyde suggests, still has a slightly 'infra-dig' reputation. Many patients, he says, come because their families have always been treated herbally while others come on recommendation or because they have been told by their doctors that 'you'll have to live with it'. 'I start most cases at rock bottom. They've tried everything by the time they get to me. I often think how much easier my job would be if they came to me first.' He begins by a lengthy interview noting the patient's health history in great detail, including apparently trivial childhood illnesses. 'You can never have too much information about a patient.' Most patients are in need of dietary guidance and strict observance is essential to give herbal medicine a chance to work. The Hyde Clinic's dispensary makes up and despatches herbal medicine only for patients who attend in person. Most herbal medicines are composite treatments made up from a number of herbal tinctures diluted with distilled water.

Does Herbal Medicine Work?

This question is frequently asked of herbal practitioners and they invariably answer it by pointing out that plant medicines are more widely used throughout the world than any other form of treatment; this would not happen, they say, if herbal medicine was ineffective. Herbal practitioners in Britain are cautious about making claims for the success of their treatments, but they believe that their record compares favourably with orthodox medicine. They mostly adhere to the orthodox definition of a 'cure': five years without recurrence of symptoms. It is probable that not a high proportion of cases comes into the category of 'totally cured', but all practitioners can cite patients who made remarkable recoveries from serious illness.

A man suffering from leaking heart valves consulted a herbalist after being told by a surgeon that he would not survive an operation to correct the problem and that he had only a year to live. He was given herbal treatment designed to slow down the heart rate. After about six months he presented himself again to the surgeon who was surprised to discover not only that he had

A modern herbal practitioner in consultation with a patient.

The herbal practitioner can choose from a wide range of herbal remedies derived from plant materials prepared in solution as tinctures.

survived, but that he was well enough to undergo the operation. The patient firmly believes that his life was saved by a combination of alternative and orthodox medicine. This case represents an ideal for all alternative practitioners: herbal treatment, with its gentle strengthening effects, allied to superb modern medicine.

Herbal practitioners are puzzled by the unwillingness of most orthodox doctors even to examine plant medicine. Herbal practitioners know that they can never replace the conventional doctor, but they believe that they have something to offer in cases which have defeated conventional treatment. Scientific medicine views herbalism as a curiosity of scant interest. Many doctors feel that if there were any value in herbs, medical science would have already discovered their active ingredients and the drug industry would, by now, have synthesised them and improved them. This view is not shared by doctors in other countries comparable to Britain. In West Germany, herbal medicine occupies a respected position alongside orthodox medicine within the health care system. There is a centuries-old tradition of herbal treatment in rural France, and in Italy herbalism is widely practised and is taught as part of the pharmacological degree course at the University of Siena. Herbal remedies are sold over the counter in pharmacies in Eastern European countries. In Russia scientists are believed to be examining the medicinal properties of a wide variety of plants. In the west the leading centres for research into herbal medicine are at the University of Illinois and at Harvard; there, researchers are attempting to identify the medicinal properties of all plants known to man.

Herbal medicine does work, but it works slowly. It is partly for this reason that it has been relegated to the position of an 'alternative' when less than a century ago it was the prevailing orthodoxy. The chemical drug industry arose and became internationally powerful not simply because research chemists found ways of synthesising the medicinal action of plants, but because the twentieth century demanded quick cures. Herbal medicine with its cumulative action, helping the body to repair itself, was seen increasingly to belong to a bygone age.

But gentle treatment is often what illnesses require; the sledge-hammer approach of modern drug medicine can complicate the illness, and cause further problems which often require additional drug treatment. It is now known that iatrogenic (or drug-induced) illness is responsible for an alarmingly high proportion of hospital admissions in Britain and America. Iatrogenic illness is very unlikely to result from herbal treatment, says Nalda Gosling, a practising herbalist and former President of the National Institute of Medical Herbalists. Orthodox drugs can lead to illness even when they are given in the correct dose. Side-effects only occur in herbal medicine after a considerable overdose.

Herbalists claim that few complaints, commonly treated by doctors, would fail to respond to herbal treatment. They do not, however, claim to have all the answers, and no responsible herbalist would continue treating a patient for whom herbal treatment was clearly inappropriate. John Hyde believes herbal treatment often proves itself superior to orthodox treatment for chronic complaints. 'Because modern medicine is symptom-based, herbalism can often help in cases of arthritis, rheumatic diseases, high blood pressure, eczema, allergy problems, digestive difficulties, ulcers and many stress-related complaints. There are many herbal tranquillisers and sedative herbs which will not turn people into zombies.'

What's in a Herb?

All plants are of a complex biological and chemical structure. The efficacy of a medicinal plant derives from the active ingredient it contains although it is now accepted that the presence of many other substances in minute quantities in the plant are essential to the overall therapeutic effect. Most commonly, the active ingredients of medicinal plants are alkaloids and glycosides. Thousands of alkaloids have been discovered all of which contain nitrogen; they are found in such plants as the Poppy, Deadly Nightshade and Dogbane. Alkaloids yield powerful medicines such as morphine, atrophine, cocaine and quinine. Glycosides are compounds whose active parts are bound to a sugar, often glucose. One of the most important is the leading herbal heart remedy, *digitalis* or Foxglove.

The story of digitalis is often cited by herbalists to support

33

Chamomile. Chamomile tea, made from the flowers, is used as an aid to digestion

The foxglove (digitalis). The leaves contain powerful and dangerous heart stimulants.

Opium poppy capsules. The poppy is the source of many sedatives used in conventional medicine.

Belladonna. The poisonous berries are prepared and used a a sedative by herbal practitioners.

their assertion that modern drug manufacture is at fault in by-passing the complex natural chemistry of plants by extracting or synthesising only the active constituent. Increasingly, this view is receiving support from scientists working in the field of pharmacognosy and phytochemistry. Digitalis as a heart stimulant was first examined in 1775 by a Birmingham physician, Dr William Withering, who later wrote *An Account of The Foxglove*. Until the early twentieth century a medicine made from the whole leaves of the foxglove was the first-choice treatment for heart failure; it was an effective medicine, but fatal accidents were not uncommon due to the difficulty of assessing the correct dose. Digitalis is now most often prescribed as digoxin which is isolated from the plant, but Withering's recommendation that the whole leaf be used has not been discounted since additional compounds in the leaf appear to complement the effects of the active ingredient.

The folklore of plants and plant medicine is another area that is beginning to interest scientists after years of ridiculing herbalists' mumbo-jumbo. For example, the old herbalists knew from trial and error that the time of harvesting was significant to the effectiveness of the plant as a medicine. It is now accepted that the morphine content of the poppy is higher at 11 am than at 3 pm. More and more plants are being found to vary in the level of their active ingredients according to the time of day and the season of the year. One such plant is the stinging nettle which our forefathers gathered as the ingredient of soup until midsummer when the chemistry of the plant changed to give it laxative properties.

Professor James Fairbairn of the Pharmacognosy Department of the University of London believes that an understanding of synergistic action – the way constituents of plants interrelate chemically and biologically – is essential to an effective evaluation of their therapeutic value. Professor Fairbairn, in a recent experiment, compared crude cannabis with its active constituent, tetra-hydra-cannabinol or THC, and found that the sedative and tranquillising effects of the crude material were about four times stronger than the isolated ingredient. Professor Fairbairn believes scientists have, until recently, tended to ignore the possibility that the whole plant might be therapeutically more effective. Much research time and money was spent, says Professor Fairbairn, to find a method of extracting the active ingredient from senna, the ancient laxative. But the active ingredients, particularly sennacide, were found to be unstable, and it became clear that the extraction method could never become commercially viable. The researchers eventually decided to make tablets from the whole senna plant by the old-fashioned method of reducing the dried plant to powder and compressing it. The resulting chemically standardised tablets were found to be 50 per cent stronger than the isolated ingredient. 'Herbal remedies went out of favour,' says Professor Fairbairn, 'because physicians could not be certain that they were giving the correct dose. One herbalist's method would yield a weak or ineffective dose while another's would be far too strong.' Because some crude material can now be standardised, Professor Fairbairn believes that there may be a future for other herbal medicines derived from the whole plant. 'We have come full circle because only now are we beginning to realise that perhaps the ancient medicine men and their methods do have something to teach us.'

Herbal Self-treatment

Herbal medicine has traditionally relied on herbs and plants which are easily available, and particularly on those that can be prepared at home, usually in the form of an infusion. To make an infusion, herbalists usually recommend one ounce of the herb to one pint of boiling water, or a proportion of those quantities. Leave to infuse in the pot for five to ten minutes.

The following list of herbs and their uses has been compiled by Hein Zeylstra, Director of Education at the National Institute of Medical Herbalists. They can all be gathered wild or cultivated; they can also be bought dried from health food or herbal shops, and by mail order. All can be used to make an infusion.

Herbal treatments do not offer an instant cure for any complaint; they are mostly slow-acting remedies, and should be given a trial of some weeks. Only one herb, juniper, is toxic in a high dose, but care is advisable when making any herbal remedy.

AGRIMONY: Chronic dyspepsia or indigestion; diarrhoea.

CHAMOMILE: Diarrhoea; gastritis; colitis; migraine.

COLTSFOOT: Coughs; bronchitis.

COMFREY: Skin complaints; healing agent for bruises, wounds and sprains.

DANDELION: *Root* is used for liver disorders; stimulates flow of bile; rheumatic complaints.
Dandelion *leaves* are an excellent diuretic; gout; rheumatic conditions; skin disorders.

ELDERFLOWER: Colds; fevers; catarrh; sinusitis and other respiratory complaints.

FENNEL: Flatulence and dyspepsia.

GARLIC: High blood pressure; increases resistance to infection.

HOPS: Insomnia; hyperactivity; aphrodisiac for males.

JUNIPER: Cystitis and other urinary tract complaints. NB: Juniper berries can be toxic in large doses.

LEMON BALM: Nervous heart complaints; palpitations; herbal tranquilliser.

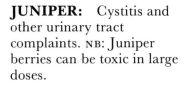

MARIGOLD: Usually used externally in lotions and creams for abrasions, bruises and ulcers.

MARSHMALLOW: Specific for peptic and duodenal ulcers; cystitis; catarrh.

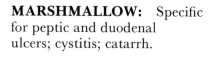

NETTLE: Skin disorders; diuretic; anaemia.

PEPPERMINT: Indigestion; stomach cramps; colic; colds.

ROSEMARY: Stimulates circulation; rheumatism.

SAGE: Excellent mouthwash; gargle for sore throats; helps control perspiration; also stops milk flow when children are being weaned.

THYME: General inflammatory conditions; coughs; bronchitis.

VALERIAN: Nervous tension; headaches; migraine; insomnia.

YARROW: General fevers; colds; lowers heart rate; diuretic.

भारत INDIA

Chinchona bark was to Hahnemann what the falling apple was to Newton and the swinging lamp to Galileo

२.०० *२००*

XXXII अंतर्राष्ट्रीय होम्योपैथिक कांग्रेस
XXXII INTERNATIONAL HOMOEOPATHIC CONGRESS

India, where homeopathy still thrives, acknowledges its debt to Samuel Hahnemann with this commemorative postage stamp.

Homoeopathy

Illness arises by similar things,
and by similar things can the sick be made well.

Hippocrates

Homoeopathy is perhaps more scoffed at by members of the orthodox medical profession than any of the other leading alternative therapies. It is ridiculed by people who have had a conventional scientific training because homoeopathy cannot be explained in terms of pure science.

Homoeopathy rests on two principles. First, that illness can be cured by giving a minute dose of a substance which, given to a healthy person in a substantial dose, would produce symptoms similar to those of the illness being treated. Secondly, that homoeopathic remedies become stronger the more dilute they are.

The word *homoeopathy* derives from two Greek words: *homoios* meaning *similar* and *pathos* meaning *suffering*. The theory on which homoeopathy is based – the law of similars – was current in the time of Hippocrates who in the fourth century wrote: 'Illness arises by similar things, and by similar things can the sick be made well'. But it was not until the late eighteenth century that a system of medical treatment – homoeopathy – was founded upon it.

Homoeopathy was developed in Germany about 170 years ago by Christian Friedrich Samuel Hahnemann. Hahnemann was born in the Bavarian town of Meissen in 1755, the son of a porcelain painter. He was a precocious child, proficient in botany, mathematics, and languages; he was able to teach Latin and Greek at an age when other boys were struggling with first principles. He later claimed that his intellectual abilities had been enhanced by his father's practice of giving him 'thinking problems' and making him remain in a room until he had reached a solution.

Samuel Hahnemann (1755–1843), the founder of homeopathy.

After leaving school Hahnemann studied medicine, first at Leipzig and later in Vienna, then the Mecca of all European medical students. He qualified as a doctor in 1779 and for nearly twenty years he practised as a physician in Hungary and in Germany. But by his mid-thirties he was so disturbed by the medical methods of his day – the blood-letting, the purging, and the barbaric treatment of mental patients – that he decided to give up the practice of medicine.

By the time of his 'retirement' Hahnemann had created for himself a formidable reputation as a physician, chemist and writer on medical and scientific matters. Since his schooldays he had never wholly given up his interest in languages, a facility he now relied upon to support himself and his wife and five children.

Hahnemann hit on the underlying principle of homoeopathy while translating *Materia Medica* by Professor William Cullen of Edinburgh University. Cullen stated that the standard cure for malaria or the ague was *Cinchona* or Peruvian bark. But Hahnemann knew that the workers who harvested the bark, the source of quinine, often became ill, displaying all the symptoms of malaria. Now why, Hahnemann asked himself, did a substance that was known to cure malaria also seem to cause it? He decided to observe the effect of the bark on himself.

For several days he took a small quantity of Peruvian bark twice a day. This was both imaginative and courageous because Hahnemann well knew that the bark in high doses could cause nausea, deafness, and other unpleasant side-effects. Professor Cullen had stated that the bark cured the ague because of its 'tonic effect on the stomach'. Hahnemann argued that other substances, more powerful than Peruvian bark, had a similar action on the stomach, but did not cure the ague. So the question that he wanted to answer was this: what did the Peruvian bark do, and how did it do it?

After the first week of this crude clinical trial, Hahnemann found that he had induced in himself all the symptoms of malaria, a disease he was familiar with from his early medical practice in the marshlands of Hungary. The experiment showed that Peruvian bark which cured malaria could also induce malarial symptoms in a healthy person. But there was a long way to go before homoeopathy could exist as a system of medicine. For the next twenty years Hahnemann carried out similar experiments with other substances.

In 1810 he published the results of what he called his 'provings', and also his theory of homoeopathy in the *Organon of the Rational Art of Healing*. Two years later Hahnemann was able to demonstrate the practical application of homoeopathy. Napoleon's army was retreating defeated, starving and disease ridden across Europe when, after the brief Battle of Leipzig in 1813, an epidemic of typhoid broke out. Hahnemann treated 180 cases of which only one died.

The remaining decades of the nineteenth century saw homoeopathy established in many countries. It was enthusiastically taken up in the United States; where by the end of the century, there were some seventy homoeopathic hospitals. Hahnemann was considered enough of a benefactor to mankind for a grand monument to be erected to his work and memory in central Washington.

Hahnemann's attractive theories brought many doctors to study under him. Among them was a London physician, Frederick Foster Quin, who set up as a homoeopath in 1832. Six years later he was instrumental in founding the Homoeopathic Hospital in London's Golden Square. Homoeopathy, then as now, attracted much irrational comment; the medical orthodoxy did not welcome the new therapy and wanted to stamp it out before it had a chance of establishing itself. The pharmacists feared it because they believed that ány doctor who prescribed minimum doses must be an arch-enemy. Quin was soon embattled, defending homoeopathy from the snipers and the envious. Then, as with Hahnemann's experience with Napoleon's army, a tragic event provided an opportunity for homoeopathy to be seen to be unmistakably effective.

In 1854 London was hit by an outbreak of cholera and the Homoeopathic Hospital was one of several hospitals given over to treat the disease. While other hospitals were losing 52 per cent of their patients, the mortality rate at the Homoeopathic Hospital was 16 per cent. Despite this impressive evidence, Quin had to fight for the inclusion of these statistics in the official records; later he was to campaign successfully for the right of homoeopathic doctors to practise legally in Britain.

Quin's victory undoubtedly introduced what can now be seen as the heyday of homoeopathy. It was to retain its popularity throughout the remainder of the nineteenth century, but its future was about to be undermined by the burgeoning chemical drug industry. If homoeopathy reached its apogee in the Edwardian age it can be said to have been in decline ever since. There can be little doubt that the possibility of total extinction in Britain was more than probable and might have occurred but for the Royal interest which began in 1893 when Princess Victoria of Teck or Queen Mary, as she became, laid the

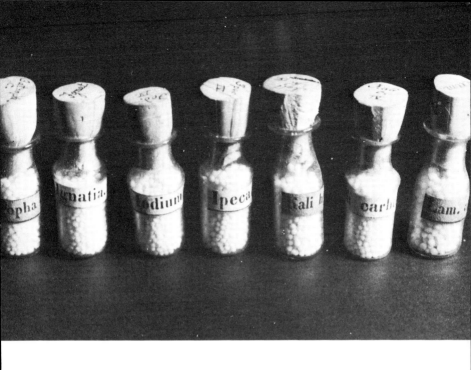

Some of the two hundred remedies in Hahnemann's medicine chest. Over two thousand are available to homoeopaths.

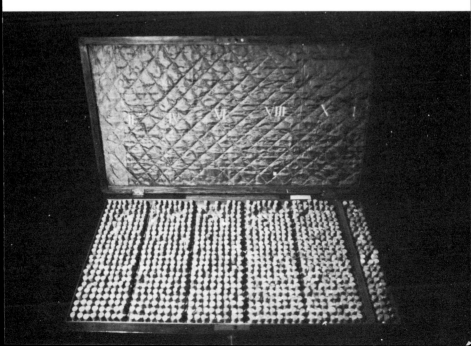

foundation stone for the new Royal London Homoeopathic Hospital.

The homoeopathic connection with the Royal Family has continued since that time. King George V appointed a homoeopathic physician. The Queen and the Queen Mother consult the Royal homoeopath when needed and Prince Charles is said to use *Arnica* ointment to treat the inevitable bruises that result from strenuous sport.

The present homoeopathic physician to the Queen is Dr Charles Elliott who succeeded Dr Margery Blackie in 1981. Dr Elliott is one of several Royal Physicians, but he alone practices unorthodox medicine. As a convinced homoeopath Dr Elliott suggests that Her Majesty's excellent health is in some part due to the Royal Family's reliance on homoeopathy during several generations although he concedes that it must also be related to her genetic background. Dr Elliott, in common with most homoeopathic doctors, recognises that the support of the Royal Family has helped keep homoeopathy alive in Britain, but he believes that its present resurgence is due to younger doctors and patients who are concerned that drug therapy is becoming increasingly risky. 'I think that in the past decade or so we have been seduced by science, but at the same time we've seen the tragedies of Thalidomide and Practilol. I think people are beginning to say enough is enough. Patients also realise that a doctor is not failing in his job if he does not prescribe a drug.'

There are about three hundred doctors practising homoeopathy, in the National Health Service or privately, in Britain today. There is also a growing number of lay homoeopaths. Lay practitioners should not necessarily be rejected out of hand. Because they are 'specialists' their knowledge of homoeopathy is often superior to that of doctors who have 'qualified' through attending a brief course at the Royal London Homoeopathic Hospital. Many homoeopathic doctors, aware that they cannot meet the increasing demand for treatment, approve of lay homoeopaths provided they and their patients realise that their prescribing is sometimes limited by their lack of medical knowledge.

Doctor-homoeopaths have for years pressed for homoeopathy to be included in the medical syllabus, but the medical

The homoeopathic pharmacist can often advise a customer about the correct remedy for a particular condition.

schools conform unwaveringly to the long-established view that homoeopathy is unproven and is therefore unworthy of inclusion in an already packed course designed to provide a scientific education.

Homoeopathy today is in a beleaguered position. The orthodox profession would shed not a tear were it to disappear overnight. The several homoeopathic hospitals around the country could, without difficulty, be absorbed into the orthodox system. Only a comparatively minor proportion of their treatment is purely homoeopathic and they are, in practice, almost indistinguishable from orthodox hospitals.

Although more doctors than ever before are 'crossing the floor' to become homoeopaths, they are still regarded as curiosities by many of their orthodox colleagues. Why, they ask, should any doctor choose to fight a war that demands tanks and missiles with swords and sidearms? For all that, homoeopathy remains a viable alternative, one that seems to appeal to increasing numbers of patients.

But what is the experience of consulting a homoeopath like and how does it differ from a visit to an orthodox general practitioner? First of all, you may find it difficult to find a homoeopath in your area, or one who is not in private practice. Whether you pay or not your first appointment will last at least an hour to enable the homoeopath thoroughly to 'take the case'.

47

You will be asked many questions, not only about the complaint, but also about your lifestyle, and your thoughts, habits, and preferences. The homoeopath is trying to build a picture of you as a person, not merely as a vehicle for an illness. He will want to know, for example, what you like to eat, whether you like to sleep with the window open or closed, whether you are hot or cold in bed, and so on. There will be many questions: are you afraid of heights, what makes you angry, are you troubled by noise, are you frightened of animals, do you like open spaces? Many of the questions will seem irrelevant, but only by finding out the answers to questions like these can the homoeopath build up a picture of you as an individual, a picture that he can then relate to a remedy.

Quite often a patient will unwittingly display relevant symptoms during a consultation. A South London homoeopath taking the case of a young girl complaining of depression and general malaise, noticed that even during hot weather when he was in his shirt sleeves the patient would remain well wrapped-up. 'This clearly meant that chilliness was a deep and significant symptom for her. We got rid of the chilliness with *carbo veg* (vegetable charcoal) which made her feel generally much better. *Aurum* (gold) saw off the depression and she made a complete recovery.'

At the end of the interview, don't expect to be handed a piece of paper to take to your nearest chemist. If the case is at all complicated the homoeopath could spend several hours attempting accurately to match the symptoms you have told him about with the entries in the various *Materia Medica*. These mighty books list the known characteristics of most of the homoeopathic remedies. It is a time-consuming task which may or may not be rewarded with success. But if the collaboration between homoeopath and patient has been open and honest the chances of success are high.

Homoeopaths describe certain remedies in terms of the people they are most likely to benefit. *Sulphur* has been called 'the ragged philosopher' because the 'provings' have shown it has a restorative effect on contemplative, rather untidy people who dislike washing and possibly have a strong odour with itchy skin and rashes. *Nux vomica*, derived from the Poison Nut, is the classic homoeopathic remedy for the irritable patient who

48

complains of the stress symptoms – poor digestion, insomnia, and headaches. *Pulsatilla* (Wind Flower) is often prescribed for people of changeable temperament, the kind of person who moves swiftly from contentment to depression.

The essential difference between orthodox medicine and homoeopathy is that a homoeopath might treat three people who all complain of headaches with three different remedies; the orthodox doctor is more than likely to prescribe the same drug for all three patients. The homoeopath is treating the person who has a headache; he will be attempting to get to the root cause of the headache. The remedy he prescribes will not attack the symptom directly, but will trigger the body's 'vital force' to heal itself and thereby remove the headache.

After the remedy is taken, there may be a worsening of the complaint, but this usually indicates that the correct remedy has been chosen and that the healing process has begun. At this stage of the treatment the homoeopath is curious about the effect of the remedy and wants to hear from you, the patient. If you report no change in your condition, the conscientious homoeopath will spend more time going over your case notes looking for missed clues and will prescribe a different remedy. Several remedies might be tried before the correct 'match' is found.

For what complaints is homoeopathy particularly effective? Dr R. A. F. Jack, a Midlands homoeopath for over thirty years, relies on homoeopathy to treat run-of-the-mill complaints. 'It's ideal,' he says, 'for handling coughs and colds, sore throats and so on. For trivial complaints I prefer not to use powerful drugs or even antibiotics because they can have unpleasant side-effects.' Dr Jack encourages his patients to be more responsible for their own health and to treat minor illness homoeopath-ically. He supplies them with a list of about twenty remedies which cover most common ailments together with notes about their use. Dr Jack recommends that none of his patients be without at least three remedies: *Aconite*, the leading homoeopathic tranquilliser, often very effective in fevers, par-ticularly in children; *Belladonna*, another quick-acting fever remedy and *Arnica* for aches, sprains and bruises. And for teething babies he recommends *Chamomilla*; its effect is almost immediate and can be given even while the child is asleep.

Allergies often respond to homoeopathic treatment where

the conventional treatment, usually anti-histamine drugs, has either failed or been abandoned because of the severity of the side-effects. Dr Jack finds that hay fever often responds to *Allium cepa* (Red Onion) or *Euphrasia* (Eyebright). Occasionally remedies can be made to suit the allergy and this can meet with spectacular success. One of Dr Jack's patients was about to give up horse riding because of the misery he had to endure. Within minutes of reaching the stables his eyes and nose would begin to run and he would sneeze uncontrollably. Dr Jack prescribed a homoeopathic preparation made from horse dander (particles of shed skin and hair from the animal's coat). The patient was told to take the remedy some hours before riding and thereafter at intervals of several months. The remedy effected an almost complete cure; his symptoms recur but not with their former severity and can be controlled by an annual dose of the remedy.

Every homoeopath can point to spectacular successes with patients for whom conventional medicine, including surgery, has failed to work. A woman teacher from Surrey had suffered for years from cystitis; all the treatments she had been given either did not work or caused unpleasant side-effects. The first remedy given to her by a homoeopath had no effect, but she persevered and was prescribed a combination of *Sulphur* and *Cantharis* (Spanish Fly). The cystitis cleared up in a few days and the patient has been free of the complaint for over three years.

A young London actor, told by his doctor that his recovery from shingles would take about six weeks, consulted a homoeopath. Following a long exploratory interview, he was given a remedy derived from the common buttercup and was back on stage within a week, not totally cured, but certainly free from the incapacitating misery that accompanies shingles.

Now what caused these remarkable cures? What do homoeopathic remedies contain that cause them to succeed where powerful orthodox drugs have failed? The answer is that a homoeopathic remedy contains barely a trace, perhaps nothing at all, of the original substance from which it was made. If you dismiss that as poppycock then it's unlikely that the following explanation about the manufacture of homoeopathic medicine will persuade you otherwise. But put aside your pre-judices for a moment and try to understand that to a homoeopath minute means mighty.

There are over 2000 remedies currently in use by modern homoeopaths. They are derived from animal, vegetable or mineral sources; over half come from living plants. Some remedies have strange sources. *Tarentula*, for example, comes from the poison of the Cuban tarantula spider. A tarantula bite typically produces hysteria and hallucinations. Consequently it is frequently used by homoeopaths to treat fits and certain psychological conditions. *Sepia*, from the ink of the Cuttle Fish, is a favourite remedy of many homoeopaths for its tranquillising properties, particularly in women. *Lachesis*, from the bushmaster snake, is frequently prescribed for menstrual and menopausal difficulties. *Apis* (Bee-sting) is often a homoeopath's first choice to relieve or reduce any kind of swelling.

Fresh plant material, like the Carolina yellow jasmine (*Gelsemium sempervirens*), is a typical homoeopathic starting material.

The *Gelsemium* plant is mashed with an alcohol and water mixture and allowed to stand for a month. The liquid content is then separated and filtered. The resulting liquid, the *mother tincture*, is the starting point of *potentisation* (the process of serial dilution).

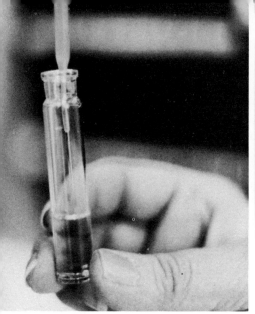

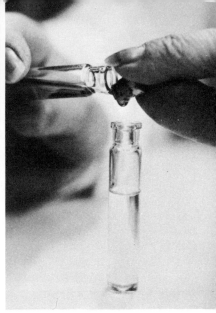

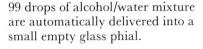

99 drops of alcohol/water mixture are automatically delivered into a small empty glass phial.

To these 99 drops, 1 drop of the original mother tincture is carefully added. This is the first centesimal dilution.

Before any substance can be used as a homoeopathic remedy it has first to be made into what is called a 'mother tincture'. In making a typical plant-based remedy the fresh material is first made into a mash together with alcohol and distilled water. To ensure complete extraction of the active ingredients in the plants the mixture is left for about a month. The liquid is then separated under pressure and filtered several times. The resulting liquid concentrate is the mother tincture. This is the starting point of the dilution process known as potentisation.

Potentisation is essentially repeated dilution. There are two methods of dilution: decimal and centesimal. The first decimal potency is made by adding one drop of mother tincture to nine drops of water and alcohol mixture. In centesimal dilution, one drop of mother tincture is added to ninety-nine drops of water and alcohol mixture. Once the first potency has been made, higher potencies are made by diluting one drop of the previous potency with a further nine or ninety-nine drops of water-alcohol mixture.

Potentisation is not complete once the first drop of mother tincture is diluted. A homoeopathic potency cannot exist until

Then the phial is placed on the succussion machine. It is shaken vigorously and struck repeatedly against a rubber pad for a few seconds. The dilution process is then repeated: One drop of this succussed phial is added to another 99 drops of alcohol/water mixture and this is then succussed.

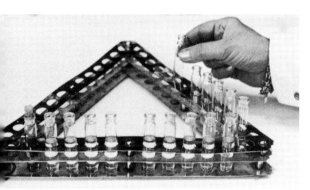

The dilution process is repeated until the required dilution strength is reached. The triangular-shaped rack has the mother tincture at the extreme left and each successive dilution is stored anti-clockwise round the rack.

Five or six drops of the required dilution are added to a bottle containing about 50 non-medicated sugar tablets. Unwanted intermediate dilutions are discarded.

the mixture has been succussed – that is, shaken vigorously for several seconds. Hahnemann stated that succussion meant not only shaking the container, but also striking it forcefully against a firm surface. Hahnemann himself used a leather-bound book, but now homoeopathic potencies are automatically succussed. This technique is thought to transfer the healing energy of the original substance to the solution.

To complete the process, a few drops of the solution are added to vials usually containing about fifty tablets. Homoeopathic manufacturers claim that all the tablets in the vial are fully medicated. It is in this form – or as pilules, granules, powders, or the mother tincture itself – that homoeopathic remedies are usually supplied.

Scientifically, of course, it just does not make sense. We all of us, scientists or not, carry around the belief that a substance, be it tea, soap, or whisky, is weaker in taste and in effect if it is diluted. To grasp the underlying basis of homoeopathy we have to allow an exception to the rule. We have to accept that in homoeopathy the more dilute the remedy the more effective it is homoeopathically. Homoeopaths also ask us to believe that although there might not be a single molecule of the original substance in the remedy – and there isn't after the twelfth dilution – it is more effective than a concentrated dose.

Production at Nelson's, Britain's leading manufacturer of homoeopathic remedies, is controlled by Jim Crawford, a qualified chemist. Why did he abandon the world of science where all phenomena are believed to be explicable, for the guesswork, surmise and intuition that seems to be the shaky underpinning of homoeopathy? It comes as no surprise to learn that he was converted after the psoriasis he suffered as a young man was successfully treated by a homoeopath. As a scientist he would welcome long-term research that might throw some 'objective light on the conundrums that bedevil homoeopathy'. For the present, he has to make the wholly unscientific assertion that 'homoeopathy works because it works'.

In the absence of objective proof, such an approach is common amongst homoeopaths. For Dr Colin Brewer, a psychiatrist who argues that both orthodox and ' fringe' practitioners tend to over-estimate their effectiveness, it will not do. 'My objection to homoeopathy is quite simply that it hasn't been shown to have any specific effect.' Dr Brewer concedes that it is a gentle treatment without dangerous side-effects. 'If it doesn't do much good,' he says, 'at least it won't do any harm.'

Dr Brewer believes that if homoeopathy wants wider and more serious acceptance it must examine its treatments from a position of scepticism. 'Why do homoeopaths, for the most part, resist the idea of controlled double-blind trials? I don't think the homoeopaths should be spared the normal standard of assessing the effectiveness of their treatments. Medicine itself has a very good track record of getting rid of ineffective treatments. Homoeopathy hasn't abandoned any aspect of its basic creed since it began and that, I think, is suspect. If evidence was produced that homoeopathy worked, I would be very happy to use it.'

Homoeopathy is not proof against criticism from within its own ranks. Dr David Lewis, a consultant paediatrician in Aberystwyth, turned to homoeopathy after years of scepticism. He believes it could and should be subjected to the double-blind trials that are standard in orthodox medicine. His interest began when his son's apparently incurable tonsillitis, which had failed to respond to conventional treatment, was cured by a homoeopathic colleague. Dr Lewis has had some encouraging results from treating eczema with homoeopathy. He recognises that the complaint fluctuates naturally, but suggests that in young children the 'placebo effect' is likely to be minimal.

One of the few independently supervised clinical trials of homoeopathy has been conducted in Scotland as a result of the enthusiasm of Dr Robin Gibson, a consultant at the Glasgow Homoeopathic Hospital. An earlier test of a group of patients with rheumatoid arthritis indicated the effectiveness of homoeopathy compared with the normal anti-inflammatory drug treatment. Encouraged by this evidence, Dr Gibson and his colleagues decided to submit their homoeopathic treatment of rheumatoid arthritis to the rigours of a 'double-blind' trial. In a double-blind trial neither the doctor nor the patients know who is being given the medicine under test.

Dr Gibson and his colleagues worked with forty-six rheumatoid arthritis patients, all of whom were allowed to continue their orthodox treatment. Twenty-three patients were given individually prescribed homoeopathic remedies while the other half received only a placebo (an ineffective dummy tablet). After three months, the condition of almost all those in the latter group had worsened whereas the patients receiving homoeopathic treatment showed significant improvement. For the second part of the trial, the placebo group was treated homoeopathically while the other active group continued to have homoeopathic treatment. After a further three months those receiving homoeopathic remedies for the first time showed a lessening of pain and marked improvement in grip-strength and mobility. Although these trials do not advance our knowledge of how or why homoeopathy works, Dr Gibson believes the results provide irrefutable evidence that homoeopathy is not, as its critics continue to claim, mere placebo.

It is only comparatively recently that homoeopathy has attracted the interest of medical and scientific researchers, but none of the projects so far completed would claim to have solved the riddle of homoeopathy. The most promising research tentatively suggests that the therapeutic energy in the original substance is imprinted on the water in which it is diluted and is then 'handed on' in successive dilutions. There is evidence that the succussion process not only assists the imprinting of the active elements in the original substance on the water molecules, but also creates a state of high energy in the remedy. Speculating, the researchers suggest that the energy in the remedy may be responsible for triggering the self-healing mechanisms in the body.

A researcher at the University of Glasgow's Physiology Department has been investigating the effect homoeopathic remedies have on leucocytes, the white blood cells which help the body to fight infection. His work shows that homoeopathic remedies do have a measurable effect on the speed at which the leucocytes attack the invading bacteria.

Homoeopathy's consumers, the patients, are not concerned with the science behind their treatment. They are like all patients of all doctors: they want to get better. They want to recover their health quickly, gently, and, if possible, naturally. They neither want nor expect their treatment to cause them further suffering. Orthodox medicine has a fine record in combating disease, but the more thoughtful members of the medical

Homoeopathic remedies are available as pilules, powders, granules, and tablets, or as mother tincture.

profession concede that its propensity to *cause* illness is now unacceptable. About 20 per cent of all hospital cases are being treated for iatrogenic or drug-induced complaints. In this area, homoeopathy has an unblemished record because a homoeopathic patient cannot develop a drug-induced illness.

It is for this and other reasons that homoeopathy appeals to Yehudi Menuhin. As President of the Hahnemann Society, one of the two homoeopathic organisations in Britain, he hopes that in time the medical profession will become more open-minded about homoeopathy. 'In health and medicine I think an exclusive approach is dangerous. Doctors should encourage homoeopathy, not try to stamp it out.' Although he acknowledges the great benefits of modern medicine he dislikes its sledge-hammer approach and much prefers the more gentle, subtler approach of homoeopathy. 'Homoeopathy is clean, harmless medicine. It encourages the patient to take part in the process of getting better.'

Self-treatment with Homoeopathy

Homoeopathic purists, like their orthodox colleagues, are mostly against self-treatment, but more enlightened practitioners encourage their patients to be more responsible for their own health.

Although homoeopathic prescribing is an individual matter – with different remedies given to different people apparently suffering from the same complaint – practitioners generally agree that many remedies for common ailments seem to work for everyone.

The following list of remedies is arranged under the complaint for which each is most suitable together with notes about the symptoms and peculiarities likely to be observed in the patient. It is based on information supplied by Dr R. A. F. Jack and the British Homoeopathic Association.

Successful homoeopathic treatment depends upon prescribing the remedy that suits the totality of the symptoms. Don't let one symptom dominate your prescribing and ignore the others. Don't let the glow of satisfaction you might feel on matching a symptom picture with a complaint blind you to the possibilities presented by other remedies. If one remedy does not work, try another. Homoeopathy is a subtle medicine and is only as good as the prescriber. And any home prescriber should guard against 'playing doctors'. Don't in your enthusiasm to 'do it yourself', continue treatment after it would have been prudent to call in a qualified medical practitioner.

Dosage Homoeopathic remedies are supplied as tablets, pilules, granules, powders or tincture. They can be obtained from any homoeopathic pharmacy (several have a postal service) and some health-food shops.

For common ailments homoeopaths usually prescribe remedies in the sixth or thirtieth potency, e.g. *Arsenicum alb 6* or *Nux vomica 30*.

Tablets contained in a small glass vial are the most convenient. One tablet of the sixth potency should be taken every two hours while the symptoms are acute and three times a day thereafter. Tablets of the thirtieth potency should be taken less frequently – say, three times a day.

Homoeopathic remedies have no harmful side-effects, but may occasionally worsen a patient's condition. This usually means that the remedy is the correct one, because patients often get worse before they get better. Treatment can then be discontinued but should be resumed if the symptoms return.

Homoeopathic remedies tend to be antidoted by strong coffee and most brands of toothpaste. Store remedies away from other products containing Camphor, Eucalyptus and Menthol.

Colds and Infections

Aconite (Aconite) Symptoms: Onset of colds, coughs, flu, and fevers often following exposure to cold wind or draughts. Patient might be fearful, trembling, or breathless; also restless and often acutely thirsty.

Camphor (Camphor) Symptoms: Feelings of being 'frozen'; sneezing; diarrhoea; symptoms partially relieved by warmth. N.B. This remedy should be stored apart from other homoeopathic medicines because camphor renders all other homoeopathic remedies inactive.

Gelsemium (Yellow Jasmine)   Symptoms: Homoeopathy's flu remedy. Use when feeling hot, flushed, aching, trembling, dizzy, drowsy or weak. Other symptoms include: headache, heaviness in limbs, chilly back, sneezing, runny nose, sore throat, difficulty in swallowing. No thirst.

Belladonna (Deadly Nightshade)   Symptoms: Flushed face, hot, shiny eyes, delirious, throbbing sensations, headache, earache. Thirsty but won't drink. This remedy often has an almost miraculous effect on children suffering from fever. Often valuable in treatment of sunstroke.

Bryonia (Wild hops)   Symptoms: Splitting headache; symptoms made worse by movement. Patient prefers to be lying down, cool, and alone, dislikes warmth. Irritable; constipated. Wants cold drinks.

Natrum mur (Common salt)   Symptoms: Sneezing, fever, blisters around nose and mouth, chapped skin, catarrh, runny nose. Chilly but worse in warm room. Craves salt; thirsty; greasy skin.

Nux vomica (Poison nut)   Symptoms: Irritable, fussy, sensitive to draughts; takes cold easily; sore throat; indigestion; colic; stomach spasms; constipation. Likes spicy, fatty, rich food; fond of alcohol.

Phosphorus (Phosphorus)   Symptoms: Hoarse; throat hurts to talk; feeling of tightness in chest; dry cough; gastritis; vomiting; skin dry and hot. Symptoms relieved by ice-cold drinks and ice-cream; likes salty food. Phosphorus often helps tall, slim, sensitive, easily fatigued people with fair or red hair.

Digestion

Carbo veg (Vegetable charcoal)   Symptoms: Dyspepsia; bloated sensation in upper abdomen; belching. Can offset effects of eating bad food. Patient feels cold, but needs to breathe fresh air.

Ipecacuanha (Ipecacuanha root)   Symptoms: Vomiting with continual nausea; wheezing and possibly leading to nosebleeds. Coughing. Clean, uncoated, pink tongue. Onset of bronchitis or whooping cough in children; no thirst.

Colocynth (Bitter cucumber)   Symptoms: Colic following anger;

relieved by bending double, warmth, pressure, and movement.

Arsenicum album (Arsenic trioxide)   Symptoms: Upset stomach from overeating or food poisoning; simultaneous diarrhoea and vomiting. Symptoms worse from midnight – 3 am; nocturnal aggravation typical of patient requiring this remedy. Fussy; chilly people; thirst for frequent warm drinks; anxious; restless.

Lycopodium (Club Moss)   Symptoms: Dyspepsia; bloated lower abdomen; belching; abdominal discomfort sometimes within minutes of eating; symptoms worse between 4 and 8 pm; suits conscientious, worrying types who like very hot drinks.

Injuries, Accidents, and Burns

Arnica (Leopard's Bane)   Symptoms: Bruises, sprains, concussion, accident injuries; muscle exhaustion from over-exertion. Arnica is available as a lotion and an ointment, but must not be applied direct to broken skin. Some homoeopaths claim arnica additionally relieves bruised feelings!

Calendula (Marigold)   Used as a lotion, ointment, or cream for rapid healing of skin wounds.

Urtica urens (Stinging nettle)   Symptoms: Any burn, however caused; also burning sensation on skin not caused by external burn, ie skin allergy. Diluted tincture applied immediately after burn brings about almost immediate relief; reinforce with internal dose.

Cantharis (Spanish fly)   Symptoms: Similar to Urtica urens. Effective for scalds from steam or water and sunburn. More frequently used as a remedy for cystitis; burning sensation in urethra.

Back Complaints

Rhus tox (Poison Ivy)   Symptoms: Backache; stiffness in joints; rheumatism, sciatica, strains and sprains. All symptoms worse in wet weather or damp conditions. Movement relieves pain as does hot bath. Tongue often coated white with red triangle at the tip.

Ruta grav (Bitterwort)   Symptoms: Ruta is an injury remedy for

61

strained ligaments, joints, tendons and areas of the body where there is little skin covering – knees, elbows, ankles, wrists. A valuable aid for sports injuries.

Hypericum (St John's Wort) Symptoms: Painful penetrating wounds from splinters, thorns or treading on nails. If there is a risk of tetanus after an accident, have an orthodox injection. Hypericum can often relieve pains in the tail-bone that might not answer to one of the other back remedies.

Children's Aches

Chamomilla (German Chamomile) Symptoms: Teething in babies; toothache; earache; any unbearable pain often allied with uncontrollable anger. Stools often spinach green; contrariness in children, irrationality.

Insomnia

Coffea (Unroasted coffee) Symptoms: Worry; active mind; agitated by the present or the future.

Opium (Opium) Symptoms: Sleep interrupted by the slightest sound, near or far; feels sleepy, but sleep does not come; restlessness.

   N.B. Lack of sleep may itself be a symptom of a more serious complaint and merits proper investigation.

Menstrual Complaints

Pulsatilla (Wind Flower) Symptoms: Weepy; changeable temperament; needs sympathy and understanding; affectionate; cannot bear heat or stuffy rooms; improved by fresh air; likes rich or fatty foods, but is upset by them. Periods suppressed or delayed or scanty yet protracted. Menopausal.

Sepia (ink of the cuttle fish) Symptoms: Periods suppressed or delayed; menopausal; morning sickness in pregnancy; dragging feeling in area of womb; weepy; brown discolouration of facial skin, often with a 'saddle' across the bridge of the nose;

likes any exercise which stimulates circulation; fearful and easily depressed.

Acne and Eczema

Graphites (Plumbago)   Symptoms: Cracks in skin at the mouth, ears, fingers. Sticky discharge; suits chilly, overweight, constipated people.
Petroleum (Crude rock oil)   Symptoms: Cracked skin; watery discharge. Eczema often responds to one of the above remedies with external application of Calendula lotion or ointment.

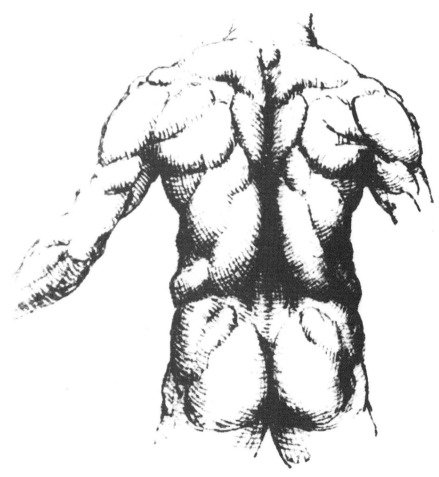

The complex musculature of the back drawn by Leonardo da Vinci.

Osteopathy and Chiropractic

> It is most necessary to know the nature
> of the spine, what its natural purposes are, for
> such a knowledge will be requisite for many
> diseases.
>
> Hippocrates

Are you sitting comfortably? Perhaps you're slouched in an armchair, or propped up in bed, or stretched out on the beach. You may be enjoying yourself, but is your spine? Is it being treated with the degree of care that this complex piece of sensitive but rugged equipment deserves? Most of us don't really bother with our backs until – usually suddenly – it doesn't seem to work. It becomes stiff, or it aches, or it develops a general or specific pain. For most of us it works away uncomplainingly despite daily abuse, until it decides that enough is enough and passes the message to its owner usually in a way that cannot be ignored.

If you have back trouble you are a member of a club with a massive worldwide membership. It's been estimated that eight out of ten people will suffer from back trouble during their lives. More of us go to the doctor about backache than any other complaint.

In Britain, about half a million people each year 'go sick' with back pain. The statistics are stark enough: about 12 million working days lost with output decreased by a staggering £220 million; social security and sickness benefits pushes the overall cost even higher.

On the face of it, these figures confirm that backache is a serious and expensive problem in the late twentieth century. But on another level they represent human misery, ranging from temporary discomfort to excruciating pain requiring powerful analgesics or major surgery on a scale that is surely unacceptable. If the wage-earner is affected his or her dependants will suffer because back trouble invariably means a spell away from work; another member of the family may have to

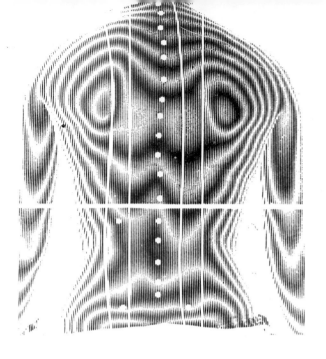

Contour photographs of the back: Each curved white line represents a contour of 1 cm. height. The white dots mark the position of each vertebra. Above: the normal back of a nineteen year old. Below: a substantial twist in the spine of a twelve year old. Surprisingly, even twists as severe as this may not necessarily produce back pain.

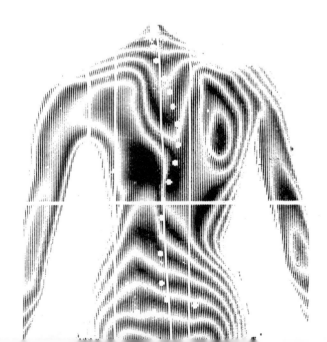

tend the patient and make up any financial shortfall.

We are becoming more sedentary. We sit down for long periods at work and at play. No doubt we could avoid much back trouble if we were more active, but we must live in the world as we find it. Production lines require large numbers of people to sit for hours at a time doing repetitive jobs which for some will eventually result in back pain. And as the so-called benefits of modern life – convenience foods, consumer goods, television and mass production – reach more and more of us we are putting our legs, and therefore our spines, into retirement. The predictable result of this worldwide inactivity is backache of almost epidemic proportions.

We no longer have to draw our water, hew our wood, or hunt for food. But did these activities, concerned with basic human existence, keep the ancient back in good working order? Bending and stretching naturally and without undue strain undoubtedly maintains flexibility in the spine. Lacking mechanical aids, our ancestors probably pulled, lifted, and pushed heavy objects excessively and injured their backs. It is evident from skeletons of ancient man that he would have spoken words equivalent to 'My back is killing me'. Back trouble is not simply a modern problem and neither is it confined to humans. In the Natural History Museum in London there are spines from horses, dogs, bears and other animals all of which show evidence of back trouble.

The spine: an engineering marvel The spine consists of 24 bone segments or vertebrae which are joined together by elastic material known as ligaments. The vertebrae are separated and cushioned by discs which are roughly similar to the cartilage which does the same job at other joints of the body. Imagine the disc, which has no blood supply and no nerve endings, as a piece of sodden leather surrounding a softer centre with the consistency of jelly. Contained and protected within this beautifully engineered structure is the spinal cord which is the main link between the brain and other parts of the body. When its importance to the body is considered it's perhaps not surprising that two systems of spinal treatment – osteopathy and chiropractic – should have been built on the belief that the spine is of overriding importance to the health of the whole body.

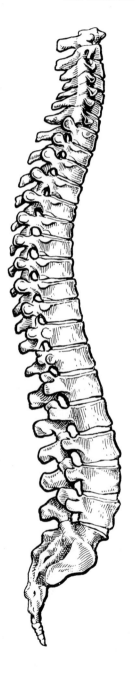

Osteopathy

Osteopathy was established in 1876 as an alternative system of medicine by an American physician, Dr Andrew Taylor Still. Still had undergone the harrowing experience of seeing three of his sons die from meningitis. Medicine had been beaten and he, its representative, was the loser.

Activated by this personal tragedy, Still set out to discover what happened to the body when it succumbed to an illness. An ex-engineer, he began by observing the mechanical functioning. His earliest conclusion was that overall health of the body depended on maintaining an uninterrupted supply of pure blood to the nervous system. Still claimed that if the circulation of the blood is normal, 'disease cannot develop because our blood is capable of manufacturing all the necessary substances to maintain natural immunity against disease'. We should remember that Still began his research at a time when scientific medicine had hardly begun; there were no X-rays, medicines were still largely derived from herbs, and the germ theory was rapidly becoming the new medical orthodoxy. Still eventually arrived at the belief, one that sustains osteopathy to this day, that the structure of the body governs its function. He derived the name of the 'new science' from the Greek words *osteos* (bone) and *pathos* (disease).

It is now firmly established in the public mind that osteopaths treat back trouble. Some osteopaths, however, claim that spinal manipulation can often alleviate asthma, migraine headaches, and abnormalities in the digestive

The human spine (viewed from the side) a marvel of engineering.

system. It is not uncommon for a patient to report after manipulation that, in addition to the back pain being relieved, sleep has improved or some other part of the body has benefited from the treatment.

London osteopath Barrie Savory tells of a young woman suffering from severe earaches who was referred to him by a doctor who had been unable to find the cause of her trouble but who suspected that it might be related to the spine. 'I examined her and found that there was a slight misalignment at the very top of the spine where it becomes the neck. I corrected it for her and within an hour the whole symptom picture of earache had gone. Had she not been sent to me it's very likely she would have gone the rounds of the ear specialists who would have found nothing at all. The doctor recognised it as an osteopathic problem.'

Such a case tends to prove the validity of Still's concept of the osteopathic lesion. A lesion in medical terms usually means some malfunction or abnormality in the body, often at a joint. Still's theory rested on his claim that the body could suffer from what he called a Total Lesion. A Total Lesion occurred when a body suffered structural, biochemic and psychological disturb-

Andrew Taylor Still
(1828–1912), the founder of
osteopathy.

ance simultaneously. The threefold treatment required to correct these imbalances Still dubbed the Total Adjustment.

It would be misleading to give the impression that osteopaths rely with total commitment on the perhaps inflated claims of the founder of osteopathy or that his teachings continue to rule their practice. To most osteopaths Still is as remote a figure and about as relevant as Lister or Hippocrates is to a conventional doctor. Where modern practitioners part company with Still most fundamentally is with the notion that osteopathy offers a system of 'whole medicine'. Of course, there are purist osteopaths who adhere to Still with the tenacity of religious fanatics, but most osteopaths, while not challenging the idea that osteopathy has a generally improving effect on the body, regard themselves disparagingly as body mechanics. It would be unrealistic of them to claim otherwise because the majority of patients go to them with some form of mechanical malfunction.

Chiropractic

In 1895, chiropractic, the creation of Daniel David Palmer, arose as an alternative system of spinal manipulation distinct from osteopathy, but with the broadly similar aim of benefiting the whole body. Palmer, a Canadian, was a magnetic healer who practised with considerable success in towns along the Mississippi. He claimed that his technique derived from the theories of Anton Mesmer who believed that there was a healing force which could be transmitted from person to person as if by magnetism, but in reality Palmer was a hand-healer who used the traditional methods of stroking and touching.

Palmer claimed to have stumbled on chiropractic when he treated the caretaker of the building in which he worked. The man had lost his hearing seventeen years earlier after exerting himself at work; he recalled that at the time he suffered a short, sharp pain in his back. Palmer, after examining the man and finding a misplaced vertebra, guessed that this might be the cause of the man's deafness. He decided against the gentle 'laying on of hands', but instead applied a sudden thrust to the man's back in the area of the original pain. Soon afterwards the

Daniel David Palmer
(1845–1913), the founder of
chiropractic.

man reported that his hearing had improved.

Palmer further developed his technique when he was presented with a case of heart trouble which was not responding to orthodox treatment. On examining the patient's spine he found a 'displaced vertebra pressing against the nerves which innervate the heart'. He adjusted the spine and the patient's condition immediately improved. Having stumbled on the significance of the spine, Palmer for the next ten years directed his study and his practical work to considering the question thrown up by his experiences that 'if two diseases, so dissimilar as deafness and heart trouble came from impingement, a pressure on nerves, were not other diseases due to a similar cause?'

Palmer thereafter invariably examined the spines of his patients irrespective of the complaint. He found that correcting displaced vertebra by manipulation frequently relieved complaints in other parts of the body. Palmer was convinced that he had hit on an exciting new science which he thought would revolutionise the art of healing, but he had enough knowledge of medical history to realise that he was reviving and possibly refining an ancient technique recommended by Hippocrates.

He would have been aware of osteopathy and there is evidence that he had met Andrew Taylor Still, but the findings he

71

enshrined in the book he published in 1910 were sufficient to found a new school and a fresh approach to the art of manipulation. Palmer's book contained many of his intuitive theories which have since been proved by modern investigatory methods or by our improved understanding of the causes of disease and illness. For example:

> 'We no longer believe that disease is an entity, something foreign to the body, which may enter from without, and with which we have to grasp, struggle, fight and conquer, or submit and succumb to its ravages. Disease is a disturbed condition not a thing of enmity. Disease is an abnormal performance of certain functions; the abnormal activity has its causes.'

Palmer was in no doubt that the causes arose from a disturbance of the central nervous system, which was itself caused by a displacement in the spine. With the help of a patient, an eminent Greek scholar, Palmer chose to call the new therapy 'chiropractic' meaning 'manual practice' or 'done by hand' from the Greek words *cheiro* (hand) and *practikos* (practice).

What must be the most thorough inquiry ever made into

Students practise the chiropractic 'high velocity low amplitude' thrust on rubber tyres.

chiropractic was conducted by a three-person commission, appointed by the New Zealand Government, which reported in 1979. The Commission was directed to look into chiropractic as practised in New Zealand, but in so doing, they widened their brief with the result that their report provides an engrossing overview, many aspects of which are applicable to any country where chiropractic is practised.

The report is almost wholly favourable to chiropractic and repeatedly underlines the shakiness of the orthodox medical profession's antagonism towards chiropractic. Chiropractic cannot be dismissed as an 'unscientific cult', said the Commission, and pointed out that chiropractors, unlike general practitioners, were fully trained to carry out 'spinal diagnosis and therapy at a sophisticated and refined level'. The Commission were unimpressed by the objections of the medical profession and stated firmly: 'Chiropractors should, in the public interest, be accepted as partners in the general health care system. No other health professional is as well qualified by his general training to carry out a diagnosis for spinal mechanical dysfunction or to perform spinal manual therapy.'

What is the Difference between Osteopathy and Chiropractic?

To a layman, observing osteopaths and chiropractors at work, the differences in approach and technique seem to be slight. An osteopath mostly treats the affected vertebra indirectly. By levering and twisting the body or parts of it, the osteopath places the area above and below the affected vertebra in a state of opposition or tension. By the force of his manipulative thrust simultaneously on the opposing areas he releases the tension which itself relieves the 'locked' vertebra.

Osteopaths use the term 'lesion' to describe a dysfunction of the spine. The chiropractic equivalent is the 'subluxation'. Any part of the spine or neck which is unable to perform its normal range of movement is said to be 'subluxated'. To correct the subluxation a chiropractor uses a more vigorous technique than the osteopath and treats most complaints with a 'high velocity low amplitude thrust' applied through the hands

73

directly to the subluxated vertebra.

While historical differences remain, there is considerable overlap in technique and neither practice is rigid enough to forbid leverage to chiropractors or a direct thrust to osteopaths. Chiropractors themselves claim that the essential difference today is that they make more frequent use of X-rays in the diagnosis of complaints and in monitoring their treatment. But this difference is becoming less significant and many osteopaths also regard radiology as an indispensable diagnostic tool.

Does Manipulation Work?

Most studies designed to measure the effectiveness of lay manipulators, osteopaths and chiropractors, invariably result in an impressive success rate of 60 per cent and above. Such surveys are regarded with some disdain by the medical profession either because they are 'unscientific' or that they are based only on the study of case histories.

This familiar complaint of the medical establishment continues to be given a regular airing. The publication of the New Zealand report referred to earlier prompted a curious response from the *British Medical Journal* in January 1980.

> 'Our objections to the claims of the chiropractors . . . is not a reflex reaction by a defensive, autocratic profession . . . No: what is wrong is the refusal by the . . . fringe practitioners to accept the standards of proof that medical scientists have developed in the past hundred years: not for nothing has the concept of the randomised, double-blind controlled trial been described as one of Britain's most important contributions to medicine since the war. In the case of chiropractic, for example, the fact that many patients treated by chiropractioners (sic) get better is seen as evidence enough of respectability. Yet what is the basis of some chiropractioners' readiness to treat diabetes or psoriasis by manipulation of the spine?'

Chiropractors would claim that patients consult them because of their dissatisfaction with orthodox medicine. It's

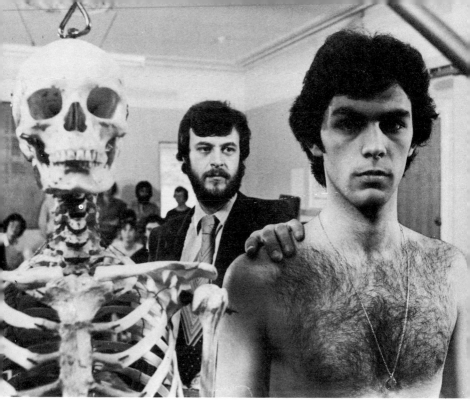

Detailed knowledge of the human musculo-skeletal system is an
essential part of the training of osteopaths and chiropractors.

now well-established that most patients of osteopaths and
chiropractors, indeed of most alternative therapies, are 'last
resort' cases which makes their success rate even more impressive. Many patients are prepared to try anything – even
spinal manipulation for psoriasis – if it offers the least possibility of a cure or relief from pain. Faced with a back problem
any manipulator would be reasonably confident of being able at
least to relieve it by manual therapy. Presented with psoriasis,
diabetes, or some other complaint apparently unrelated to the
spine, most manipulators would be guarded in their prognosti-
cation and would not hold out irresponsible hopes of being able
to improve such conditions.

The most serious charge that the orthodox profession makes
against osteopaths and chiropractors is that they lack training
and practice in the art of diagnosis. They fear that a manipulator might fail to recognise that a patient had, say, cancer of

75

the spine or neck for which manipulation would be inappropriate and possibly dangerous. The training of osteopaths and chiropractors emphasises these dangers and it is unlikely that any practitioner who had successfully completed the four year course at the British School of Osteopathy or the Anglo-European College of Chiropractic would continue to manipulate willy-nilly when radiological or other evidence suggested that the complaint would be unlikely to respond and required other treatment.

In the absence of the impossible – wholly scientific testing of osteopathy and chiropractic – we have to rely for proof of their efficacy in treating back troubles and other complaints on what medical journals refer to as 'anecdotal evidence'. Anecdotal evidence – in other words, stories about how this or that treatment cured this or that complaint – is a red rag to the medical profession particularly if it's relied on to support any claim by a 'fringe medicine'. But anecdotal evidence can be valuable. One can be dubious about a handful of stories about even remarkable cures because other factors might have had a hand in bringing about the cure, but when anecdotal evidence accumulates it must be seen in a different light. After all, we conduct much of our lives – our likes and dislikes, our reputations and those of others – on the basis of anecdotal evidence. Why, then, should it be ruled out of court when we have to decide what kind of medical treatment we shall use?

Does manipulation work? It would be misleading to suggest that manipulation is the answer to all back problems. Manipulators also have dissatisfied patients. But it is perhaps significant that physiotherapists and some doctors now more frequently employ manipulative techniques, possibly influenced by the popularity enjoyed by lay manipulators. One Surrey doctor, whose back pain patients consulted osteopaths and chiropractors, was so impressed with the results that he defected from the medical profession and became a chiropractor himself.

Why Can't Medicine Beat Backache?

Patients consult an osteopath or a chiropractor in the first instance either because it would not occur to them to consult anyone else, or out of frustration or dissatisfaction with conventional treatment. The latter group is by far the largest because orthodox medicine has no speedy and effective treatment for back complaints. That is not to blame the overworked general practitioner. If an effective drug without side-effects was available, doctors would clamour to provide it. But it does not exist and therefore the doctor when faced with yet another back pain case switches over, quite understandably, to automatic pilot and following simple tests of mobility, prescribes pain killers if warranted, bed-rest, or physiotherapy. Painkillers kill pain, but should not be taken regularly over long periods; bed-rest undoubtedly relieves back trouble, but has the important side-effect in many cases of causing financial hardship. Patients suffering from persistent back trouble will be referred to a physiotherapist, usually attached to the local hospital.

But there's a catch; one that could delay the appointment of the suffering patient with the physiotherapist who offers the most hope of relief. In most parts of the country, a doctor cannot refer a patient direct to a physiotherapist. Your doctor, much as he would like to refer your case to the local physiotherapist whom he knows will fix your back, is required to write about your case to the consultant orthopaedic surgeon to whom the physiotherapist is responsible. Letters take time, doctors and consultants are busy people, the queue of backs outside the physiotherapist's door seems never to get any shorter.

It is at this point that a back pain sufferer will consult, probably with some urgency, an osteopath or chiropractor.

Consulting a Lay Manipulator

You might be lucky enough to have a doctor who recommends or even refers you for treatment by an osteopath or chiropractor. The views of the orthodox profession on lay manipulators have changed markedly in recent years. For decades the medical establishment maintained an implacable opposition to lay manipulators so unyielding that a doctor might have been disciplined by the General Medical Council had he sent a patient to an osteopath or chiropractor. But in 1978 the restriction was withdrawn and the General Medical Council conferred tentative recognition on the former outlaws. This unex-

77

pected concession, one which applied not only to osteopaths and chiropractors but to all lay practitioners no doubt relieved the consciences of those doctors who for years had quietly been referring themselves and their patients to lay manipulators.

A doctor may now refer a patient to a qualified osteopath or chiropractor provided that control of the case remains in his hands. In practice, of course, some general practitioners are only too pleased to refer a patient, thereafter retaining only token control; some are prepared to co-operate to the extent of submitting a patient's x-rays when making a referral. Unfortunately for their patients, most general practitioners remain cautious about committing a case into the hands of a 'fringe' practitioner whom through instinct and training they would regard as a quack.

British osteopaths are also understandably cautious because of the experience of American osteopathy which today is indistinguishable from orthodox medicine. In America, osteopaths fought for parity and won. American osteopaths legally style themselves 'doctor'; they undergo a seven-year training in which manipulation is not unduly emphasised, there are osteopathic hospitals all over the United States, and osteopaths are as quick on the draw with the prescription pad as any doctor. Osteopathy, as practised in its country of origin, is no longer a drugless medicine; neither is it primarily concerned with back complaints. The American experience is unlikely to be repeated in Britain which could now claim with some justification to be the spiritual home of pure osteopathy.

So if you decide to consult a manipulator – osteopath or chiropractor – the first problem is how to find one. If your doctor won't or can't help by referring you, how can you be sure the manipulator of your choice is competent?

The organisations mentioned in the reference section will provide a list of trained practitioners. You may prefer a personal recommendation. If you mention your need to friends it's very likely that someone will come up with the name of the genius who fixed up Uncle Stan's back or sorted out Aunt Flo's troublesome neck. With this kind of recommendation it doesn't matter what qualifications are displayed. However, the safest course is to ensure that you are placing yourself in the hands of a well-qualified and experienced practitioner.

What Do Manipulators Do?

The manipulator – osteopath or chiropractor – will begin by taking a detailed medical history before putting the patient through a physical examination. He will observe the posture and stance of the patient, whether he can move his limbs, back and neck without pain or discomfort. He will be looking for any peculiarities which might give a clue to finding the site of the problem.

It may be that your work requires you to repeat a movement which over the years has caused some misalignment of the spine. Sportsmen are sometimes prone to this kind of spinal malfunction. The Olympic runner, Sebastian Coe, found that he had developed a 'pelvic tilt' as a result of always running in races and in training anti-clockwise. This discovery was made by osteopath Terry Moule of Hemel Hempstead who corrected the problem by manipulation and advising Coe to include clockwise track running in his training programmes. 'Before coming to see Terry I knew I was running slightly lop-sided

Olympic runner, Sebastian Coe, is regularly treated by Hemel Hempstead osteopath, Terry Moule.

because I was always running the same way round the track and straining my left leg. I was compensating, or over-compensating, for it and it was causing me hamstring problems and trouble in my back and neck. Terry worked on me before the Moscow Olympics and the problems stabilised for a time, but immediately after I was back to square one again.'

Terry Moule says 'pelvic tilt' is quite common in athletes of Coe's ability and, he says, over-enthusiastic joggers ought to be aware of it as a potential problem. 'In Seb's case, because of his great ability and the degree to which he pushes himself, it was a serious problem from the start. The early treatment brought a dramatic improvement, but because of training pressures it was discontinued for a time. Just before Moscow he even had difficulty in walking.'

The manipulator will next make a detailed examination of your spine feeling between and around each vertebra for any displacement. If the manipulator finds a misplaced vertebra he would normally make an adjustment to assist it to regain its correct position. It's because of the speed of diagnosis and cure that osteopaths and chiropractors have acquired their 'miracle men' reputation. One manipulation is often sufficient, but many complaints of long standing require more comprehensive treatment.

Throughout the consultation and initial examination the manipulator will be looking for and attempting to eradicate areas of tension in the body which may be the prime cause of back trouble. Osteopaths favour a combination of massage and gentle manipulation of the joints, muscles, and tendons to restore a full range of movement before attempting more vigorous manipulation. Osteopaths and chiropractors are well aware that many patients who might be helped by manipulation are reluctant to submit to treatment because they fear that it will hurt. Manipulation is not painful in the sense that a twisted ankle or a pulled muscle would feel sore. Patients often believe that they will be pulled and twisted into painful positions and that their muscles and joints will be stretched and wrenched to produce a so-called 'crack'. It is true that manipulation of the back or neck often produces an audible sound, but while this may sound thunderous to some patients, it is in reality no more than a click. Manipulation in most cases pro-

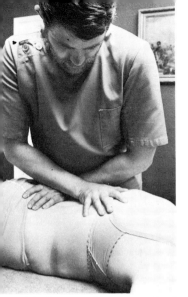

(a) Osteopaths commonly find slight misalignments at the top of the spine.

(b) The osteopath manipulates the spine in an attempt to clear any abnormality which may be the cause of present or future trouble.

duces little more than local discomfort which usually fades away after a few days as the joint becomes used to moving freely again.

By far the most common complaint presented to manipulators is *low back pain*. This is what most people think of as backache, and it originates in the lumbar spine – that is, the lower half dozen vertebrae – or in the sacro-iliac joint which is the name given to the important junction between the base of the spine and the upper bones of the legs. Osteopaths, chiropractors and orthodox physiotherapists are all agreed that most backache is due to the way we live in the twentieth century. If the body is still learning how to walk on its hind-legs it must certainly be puzzled by the ever-increasing amount of rest periods it is allowed.

But having taken with some enthusiasm to life with our feet up, we continually surprise our backs by making unreasonable demands for sudden exertion. 'You can't spend all day sitting in an office or at a workbench and then come home and start decorating your house,' says London osteopath Barrie Savory. 'Unless you're very fit your back just won't stand for it.'

The truth is that in moving rapidly from a sedentary exist-

81

ence to strenuous activity without having prepared the spine, is to abuse the back. A car that is neglected is eventually going to break down. If we don't want our backs to break down as a result of neglect we have to 'service' our backs just as we service any piece of mechanical equipment. Most osteopaths and chiropractors have a few patients who make occasional visits, say, once or twice a year, for a check-up – the equivalent of the 10,000 miles service – so that any incipient problems can be nipped in the bud.

'The problem,' says Barrie Savory, 'is that most patients don't know, until the condition's developed and they're in pain, that there's something wrong with the back. A general check-up, once a year, might have prevented it. I'm never surprised to find, when I have my own back examined, that some little problem needs correcting.'

While low back pain or backache is irritating or uncomfortable, a *slipped disc* can cause excruciating and often temporarily incapacitating pain. When we hear that someone has a slipped disc, we imagine that part of the spine which should remain in place has 'slipped' out of position. The truth is that discs do not slip. Discs are the leathery washers or shock absorbers between the vertebrae which have softer centres. What happens when a disc 'slips' is more correctly described as a hernia; the jelly-like middle area, as the result of overstrain or an accident, escapes and bulges out between the vertebra, and because it has nowhere else to go it protrudes into the spinal canal. This condition, which nearly always affects the lumbar, or lowest area of the spine, is considerably more painful than ordinary backache.

Your doctor faced with what he believes is a slipped disc will advise painkillers and bed-rest. In many cases, however, manipulation can effect speedy relief by temporarily easing the pressure on the disc thereby allowing the disc to regain its former shape and position.

Preventing Back Trouble

Osteopaths and chiropractors differ in their approach to the treatment of back complaints, but they are broadly in agreement about how to prevent them. Every day of our lives our bodies are engaged in three activities: sitting, standing, and lying. Most people who suffer from back trouble are sitting, standing or lying incorrectly.

Sitting   Modern life, at work or at play, requires many of us to sit for long periods. To sit down for say three or four hours without moving, except to lift a cup of tea or the telephone or to change gear, is asking a lot of your spine. If your job requires this of you, or you're a chess buff, think about what you're doing to your back. Trouble can often be prevented by becoming aware of what is happening to your body.

The most effective preventive measure for avoiding backache is gentle stretching exercises before and after periods of sitting down. Japanese and Chinese people suffer less back trouble than we in Britain and America, possibly because of the more or less enforced exercises with which they start their working day. We would all probably be better for such regular exercise, but it is not difficult to imagine the response of the nation's factory and office workers were such a regime made part of our working day.

Driving   Most car seats are not designed to prevent back trouble. Indeed, it's a matter of dispute amongst manipulators whether such a seat of perfection is possible. However, at least one leading car manufacturer, Mercedes Benz, consults a chiropractor about seat design with the result that an orthopaedic back-rest is available, but only as an optional extra.

In a recent survey the seats in a number of popular cars were assessed for lumbar suitability. The results largely confirmed what any driver of the average family car already knows. It was found that, with few exceptions, car seat design was skimped even in some expensive models. The report suggested that improved seat design should not increase the overall cost of the vehicle.

Since we are condemned to drive or ride in cars with built-in backache, we still can effect considerable improvement in the position of the spine by placing a small cushion in the lower or lumbar area. This will not bring a banger's seat up to Rolls

Here are a few simple rules which, if your follow them, could cut down your chances of developing backache

WRONG   RIGHT

Don't slouch around with hunched shoulders and stomach stuck out. Just stand straight and relaxed with shoulders reasonably far back, chest pushed forwards and stomach in.

When you have to pick up something heavy *always* do it with a straight back. The strain will then be transferred to your legs and you won't risk a sudden agonising pain in your back.

Always bend your knees when picking up a baby. Hold the child close to you and lift by straightening your legs. At all times, try to avoid bending, twisting, and lifting simultaneously.

Don't bend your back to make a bed, bend your knees and keep your back straight. When buying a bed, choose a good mattress which is really firm – that way your back will be properly supported every night.

84

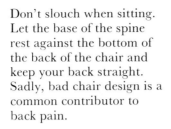

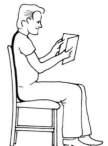

Don't slouch when sitting. Let the base of the spine rest against the bottom of the back of the chair and keep your back straight. Sadly, bad chair design is a common contributor to back pain.

When driving don't hunch over the wheel with knees sharply bent. Try to sit in an upright position and keep your legs partly extended. Bad car seat design is the norm rather than the exception. Often a small cushion at the base of the spine can improve the sitting position.

Royce standard, but your journey is guaranteed to be more comfortable. And that ache in the small of your back that most drivers experience either won't be there or it will disappear more quickly than it would have done without support.

If you do find yourself getting stiff during a long drive, pull off the road and walk about. Stiffness in the shoulders and neck while driving can be prevented, or eased, says Barrie Savory, by shrugging your shoulders once or twice every hour or so.

Standing The most common attitude we adopt when standing is to place most of the weight of the body on one leg. This is all right so long as we vary the leg taking the weight, but we don't. Either the right leg or the left leg habitually does all the work because most of us lack awareness of what we are doing with our bodies. So, vary the leg, or learn to stand on both feet with the weight evenly distributed. There is nothing formal or military about such a stance; it should be relaxed and there should be no sense of strain. If you watch football from the terraces, you'll find you're far less tired at the end of the match if

85

you adopt the even-weight stance rather than the unconscious shifting stance with the centre of gravity of your body constantly changing.

Barrie Savory also advises holding in the stomach muscles and tucking in the bottom almost as if you were trying to pack it away in the space under the lower part of the spine; neither stomach nor bottom should protrude.

Lying People claim to sleep on the left side, the right side, prone or flat on their backs, but what they mean is that they *start* sleeping in this position, but during the night the body goes through several changes of position. As position during sleep is uncontrollable, we rely on the body to find a comfortable position which does not place undue strain on the body. It's not a good idea to read for long periods propped up on pillows against a bedhead or the wall. It places your lumbar spine under considerable strain, even more so if you fall asleep in that position.

Chiropractor Ian Hutchinson believes much advertising for beds and mattresses is misleading. It is possible to pay heavily for a so-called orthopaedic bed. He believes that it is usually possible to achieve much the same effect by placing a board between the bed and the mattress. Beds that are claimed to be 'good for bad backs' usually only have a firmer base and mattress. The bed your back will like best is a simple wooden base without springs with a firm mattress of good quality. Regularly sleeping on such a bed can sometimes be a therapy of sorts for sufferers from backache.

ripigmentũ.   Inunctio olei.   Fricatio.   Bilmalua. Vel

Early methods of treating back trouble.

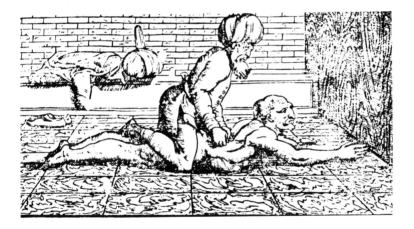

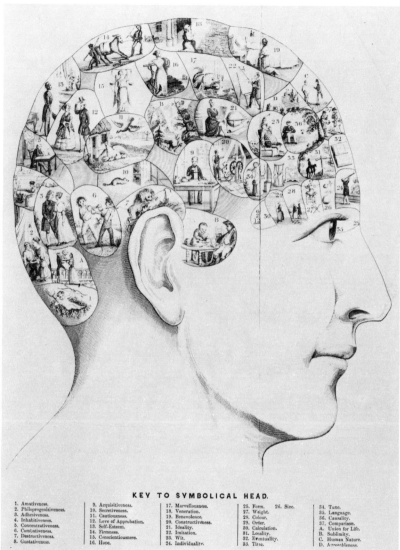

KEY TO SYMBOLICAL HEAD.

Hypnotism and Biofeedback

Much will rise again that has long been buried, and much become submerged that is held in honour today.

Horace

Hypnosis was first used as a medical therapy some three thousand years ago, but we tend to think of it more as a shabby part of show business than as an effective cure for many complaints, including allergies, phobias, bedwetting and other problems related to emotional difficulties. Hypnosis today is enjoying something of a renaissance. This is typical of its recent history, for, since the beginning of the nineteenth century, hypnosis has alternated between periods of popularity and plummeting disfavour.

Alternative medicine finds it difficult enough to gain widespread acceptance, but hypnosis has had to fight on two fronts: not only that it is unorthodox, but that its theatrical connections inhibit serious consideration. There are, however, enough medically qualified doctors practising hypnosis for it to have established a niche within the profession, one that it shares with the less fashionable areas of orthodox medicine.

Although there is evidence that hypnotism was practised by the Ancient Egyptians, the Greeks and the Romans, it was not until the second half of the eighteenth century that its use as a healing therapy began to be widely appreciated. The father of what was later called hypnotism was a medically qualified lawyer and philosopher named Franz Anton Mesmer. After seeing a healer at work in Switzerland, Mesmer concluded that healing depended on the magnetic attraction of two poles within the body. He believed that an invisible 'magnetic fluid' passed between the two poles. Illness resulted if it was interrupted and could be corrected only if it was restored. Mesmer experimented with magnets, but eventually he came to believe

89

Franz Anton
Mesmer
(1734–1815)

that his undoubted healing powers came from what he called
'animal magnetism': his ability to conduct his magnetism into
the bodies of his patients, through magnetised objects.

Mesmer's immense success had inevitable results, de-
pressingly familiar in the history of unorthodox medicine. The
Viennese medical establishment, jealous of his ability to cure
the apparently incurable, accused Mesmer of witchcraft and
'fraudulent practice' and made it impossible for him to continue his work in Vienna. He went to Paris where he continued
his work on what was now recognisably, hypnotism or auto-
suggestion.

After Mesmer's death in 1815 the study and development of
'mesmerism' continued in France and later in Britain. The
Lancet, however, attempted to throttle the fledgling therapy
with ridicule:

> 'Mesmerism is too gross a humbug to admit of any further
> notice. We regard its abettors as quacks and impostors.
> They ought to be hooted out of professional society. Any
> practitioner who sends a patient afflicted with any disease

90

to consult a mesmeric quack ought to be without patients for the rest of his days.'

This choleric demand was ignored by a leading Manchester surgeon, James Braid, who not only put down the roots of medical hypnotism in nineteenth century Britain, but also provided it with a credible theoretical basis. It was Braid who gave hypnotism its misleading name derived from the Greek *hypnos* meaning sleep, but hypnotism is not sleep. After seeing a demonstration of mesmerism in 1841 Braid began experimenting and came to believe that Mesmer's magnetic theory was nonsense. He decided that 'artificial somnambulism' or a trance state could be induced by eye fixation – on a bright object or the hypnotist's eyes – augmented by suggestion. Despite Braid's innovative work, hypnotism continued to be regarded with scepticism for the remainder of the century. A committee appointed by the British Medical Association admitted in 1891 that hypnotism was 'frequently effective', but it was not recommended for use by the medical profession. Perhaps the strongest reason why hypnotism was not widely adopted in medicine was that Freud, a poor hypnotist, abandoned it thereby delaying the obvious link between psychotherapy and hypnosis for about fifty years. Not until the middle of this century was hypnosis accorded recognition by the medical professions in Britain and the United States.

How Does Hypnotism Work?

Medical hypnotists find it difficult to provide a simple definition of hypnosis or an explanation of how it works. Most hypnotists agree, however, that hypnosis alters the state of consciousness of the subject, at the same time inducing deep relaxation. After hypnosis, most subjects describe it as a pleasurable experience; the immediate after-effects vary from drowsiness to acute awareness and improved perception. A Buckinghamshire GP who frequently employs hypnotism to help people give up smoking says that the hypnotic state is 'a transitional state between sleeping and waking. While under the influence of hypnosis the faculty of criticism is in abeyance and suggestibility is very much increased.'

Many hypnotists claim that women are better subjects than men. Why this should be so is far from clear. Certainly intelligent people with good concentration are easily hypnotised. This does not mean that strong personalities, people with a decided sense of self, or with butterfly minds, cannot be hypnotised. Of course they can, it just takes longer.

Trust in the hypnotist and a willingness to surrender control of the self is essential to successful hypnosis. It is this apparent surrender of the personality that troubles many people who might benefit from hypnosis; they cannot come to terms with losing control of themselves. They perhaps have memories of stage hypnotists who got most of their laughs from making people bray like donkeys or scratch themselves like monkeys. People understandably fear being embarrassed by a stranger; they also fear that the hypnotist might bring to the surface feelings, thoughts, and intentions which are best left buried deep in the psyche. Of course, a hypnotist would not find it difficult to manipulate the personality of a disturbed person, but it is unlikely that a hypnotist could make the average person – one who, like most of us, carries around a bundle of fears and

A Midlands stage hypnotist demonstrates the uncanny rigidity he has induced in this volunteer by placing his whole weight on the middle of her body.

phobias – act in opposition to his authentic personality.

If a hypnotist suggests that you should hit the first person you see over the head with a mallet and that person happens to be someone who has insulted you then that person may well suffer violence at your hands. But no hypnotist would suggest this and, even if he did, you would be unlikely to obey the command because your surrender is not complete; if violence is not in your nature the hypnotist probably will be unable to induce it.

Experienced hypnotherapists employ hypnosis with some caution. One London doctor-hypnotherapist frequently rejects hypnotism in favour of orthodox psychotherapy, if the patient has, say, a deep-seated psychiatric disturbance which hypnotism would be unlikely to help and might even exacerbate. He believes that indiscriminate use of hypnotism by inexperienced practitioners, which somehow always finds its way into the newspapers, frightens off many genuine patients who might be helped by hypnotism.

Beware of books which purport to teach you self-hypnosis. The subconscious mind is too delicate an instrument to play with. You may do yourself no harm, but if you are, possibly unknown to yourself, a 'natural' hypnotist you might be tempted through ignorance of the potential danger to try out your powers on suggestible people. An amateur hypnotist amused some guests at a party by hypnotising them and suggesting that on hearing a certain song they would fall asleep. During the course of the evening the hypnotist occasionally sang a few bars of the song, promptly sending several of the guests to sleep. Several weeks later one of the guests heard the song on his car radio and immediately fell asleep at the wheel. Fortunately he was with his wife who was able to stop the car. A qualified hypnotherapist had to be found to erase the post-hypnotic suggestion.

Modern Medical Hypnosis

The technique of modern medical hypnosis, or hypnotherapy, is far from frightening. Simplicity and straightforwardness are the hallmarks of a well-conducted session of hypnosis. Most hypnotists ensure that their consulting rooms are quiet, warm and comfortable. An armchair is usually provided with the hypnotist sitting beside or in front of the subject. After the subject has outlined the nature of the complaint, the hypnotist will then begin the induction process, usually by asking the subject briefly to daydream and to allow a feeling of relaxation and well-being to enter all parts of the body. If the subject finds this difficult the practitioner might ask the subject to relax various parts of the body in turn.

Induction, the process of taking a patient into an hypnotic trance, relies upon a combination of persuasion and suggestion allied to relaxation and deep concentration. It can be exhausting for the hypnotist particularly if the patient is consciously or subconsciously resisting the suggestions. Most patients, however, can be put in a trance within five to ten minutes, but after the patient has had several sessions of hypnosis and fully accepts and understands what is required, a trance can be induced on command or by the hypnotist counting from one to five. Some practitioners require the patient to look at a lamp, say, or a flower; others start by asking the patient to close his or her eyes and to imagine the eyelids becoming heavier and heavier. It should be said that medical hypnotists do not induce a trance by staring into a patient's eyes. This technique was never widely used and derives from books, plays and films in which hypnotists were invariably depicted as sinister men in bizarre clothes. Most hypnotists employ a monotonous tone of voice with little variation in pitch or volume, except when giving a command, together with the repetition of phrases like 'heavier and heavier' or 'deeper and deeper'. A typical hypnotist's 'talk-down' might go something like this:

'Your eyelids are becoming heavier and heavier. You are pleasantly relaxed. Pleasantly relaxed. Not a worry in the world. Your face and your neck are becoming relaxed. Your breathing is easy, regular. Your eyelids are very heavy now. Very heavy. You're going deeper and deeper, relaxing your whole body, from your head to your toes. Deeper and deeper. Your arms are becoming heavy. Very heavy. Heavier and heavier. Let your whole body relax. Deeper and deeper. Listen to my voice. Deeper and deeper. Heavier and heavier. You feel pleasantly relaxed. Let your body relax ... relax ... relax ... Let your mind relax ... relax ... relax ... Empty your mind of
94

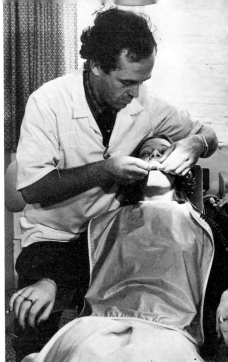

(a) A nineteenth-century tooth extraction with the patient under hypnosis.

(b) Today the patient can be kept in deep hypnosis during an operation by listening to the recorded voice of the dentist.

all thought. Deeper and deeper....'

At this point the hypnotist might check that a trance has been achieved by asking the patient to raise an arm until it is level with the shoulder. This phenomenon, known as arm levitation, will happen slowly and might take several minutes. Another common practice is for the hypnotist to instruct the patient to induce a feeling of numbness in a hand or arm and then insert a surgical needle into the self-anaesthetised skin. This is not simply an hypnotist's parlour trick; it is valuable in terms of feedback. If, say, a patient is being treated for agoraphobia, a fear of open spaces, it is likely to be psychologically helpful in strengthening the patient's resolve to overcome this irrational fear if the ability to bear pain is demonstrated.

The ability to accept and overcome pain is of considerable benefit during childbirth. Although hypnosis was first used for this purpose in 1823 it is today employed in only a few maternity hospitals. It's a time-consuming treatment which is the main reason for its limited use by obstetricians.

Dr Alfred Kozdon, an Essex general practitioner, is championing the wider use of hypnosis in childbirth. He offers hypnosis to expectant mothers in his care whom he considers it might benefit. Dr Kozdon says that most are prepared to try hypnosis, not because they are particularly adventurous about trying alternative methods, but because of all people, mothers are most concerned in these post-thalidomide days not to expose their unborn children to the risks of powerful drugs.

Dr Kozdon has trained several midwives and health visitors in the technique so that group hypnosis and instruction in self-hypnosis can take place as a regular part of ante-natal care. Expectant mothers are encouraged to understand that the control of pain is in their hands. Post-hypnotic suggestions are given to ensure that pain during the dilatation and expulsion stages of birth will be controllable by the mother.

Most of the mothers trained by Dr Kozdon or his staff say that, apart from relaxing them through their pregnancy, hyp-

A medical hypnotist tests an expectant mother's ability to bear pain under hypnosis by inserting a sterile needle into her hand. Later, at ante-natal classes, the techniques of self-hypnosis for pain relief are taught by the midwife.

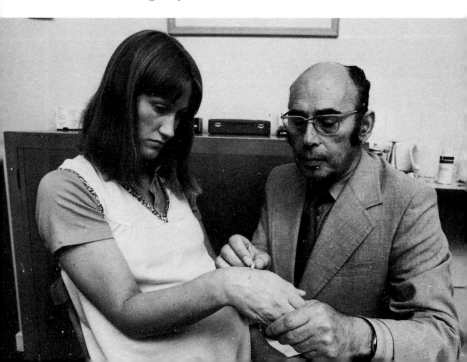

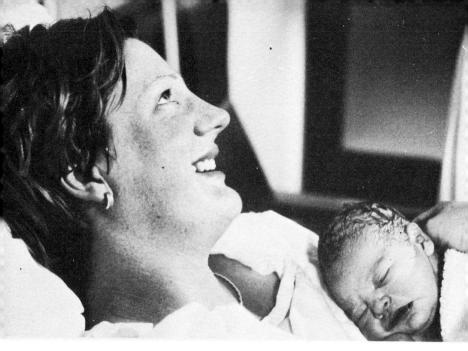

Hypnosis eases the delivery by allowing control to be maintained by the mother without resort to pain-killing drugs.

nosis gave them feelings of confidence during delivery. Although most births took place in hospital they felt that they retained control. Most important of all, they are proud to claim that they brought their children into the world, not always painlessly, but certainly without help or harm from drugs.

Like expectant mothers, sportsmen are preparing for an event. Athletes and games players are ideal subjects for hypnosis because concentration on the 'will to win', consciously or subconsciously, is a form of hypnosis.

A Surrey hypnotherapist, Eric Copperthwaite, is confident of his ability to help competitors improve their performances. If he notices that an athlete or a player has lost form he writes offering hypnotherapy. He believes that if performance in a champion athlete falls off it is almost certainly because of some psychological reason. He or she may be training just as hard as ever, but in the event the single-minded approach to winning, to beating off all opposition with the fierce determination that all champions must have, is absent. Eric Copperthwaite claims to be able to help a sportsman find and utilise the lost element in

97

his performance. He has helped several players and athletes, including the marathon runner Ian Thompson.

After a highly successful year, his best, in 1974 Ian Thompson continued to run well until 1978 when he lost the rhythm that made him a champion; he also began to suffer viral infections before big races. Ian claims that hypnotherapy helped him regain the aggressive approach to competition that he had in 1974 when running and winning seemed enjoyable. 'It is the mind that plays tricks on the body', he says, 'I felt I was somehow stopping myself from doing well.' Although Ian occasionally returns for hypnotherapy sessions with Eric Copperthwaite and also listens to tape recordings, he is not dependent on the hypnotherapist. 'He's unlocked something that I knew was there. I might have stumbled along for years trying to find what was wrong and getting nowhere. Hypnotherapy has helped me rediscover far more quickly the freshness of approach I had in my good years.'

Hypnotism is frequently used to unlock some imperative suggestion received by the patient during childhood. It may later surface in the adult and lead to disturbed behaviour. A child's mind starts as a clean slate. It takes what it is told on trust because critical faculties and objectivity are unawakened. If a child is told often enough that he is lazy he will develop a warped notion of himself and will almost certainly become what psychologists term an 'under-achiever'. Contrarily, a child of average ability can often surprise by his achievement in adult life simply because the suggestion was implanted at an early age that a certain goal was achievable.

Similarly, phobias which develop in adult life can nearly always be traced during deep hypnosis to repressed childhood experiences. Children often cope with frightening experiences they cannot understand by using a mechanism known as 're-pression'. They push the experience to the back of the mind and seal it off. But they are unable to banish it completely and it sometimes emerges later in life as an irrational fear often only loosely associated with its origin. The task of the hypnotherapist is to identify the event or experience which caused the phobia. Having done this, the patient is then able to rationalise it as an adult. Repression is no longer necessary and the symptoms it was producing disappear.

A young Essex girl was sent to a medical hypnotist because she had developed an irrational fear of birds. Walking amongst the pigeons in Trafalgar Square was impossible. To eat poultry was unimaginable. The phobia was particularly disabling when she found that she was unable to continue with her science studies at school because she could not bear to dissect a bird. In deep hypnosis the girl revealed that as a toddler she had found a bird caught behind a wire mesh drain cover. She had persuaded her parents to care for it and after a few days it seemed better and was released. The bird immediately returned behind the wire mesh and had to be rescued again. This pattern was repeated several times and eventually it died. When this experience emerged, the hypnotist, who was also a trained psychiatrist, assessed it as the girl's first experience of death. She had unconsciously continued to associate birds with death and, understandably perhaps, did her utmost to avoid them.

The hypnotist used a technique known as 'age regression'. During a deep trance the girl was told to imagine herself as a child. She was to be aware, for example, of the dress she was wearing at the age of seven, recall a favourite teacher, the school playground. The therapy continued for several weeks and at each session the girl was given the suggestion during deep hypnosis that she would no longer be afraid of birds. She was confronted with the seeds of her adult phobia – the childhood experience – and her subconscious was given the task of removing the irrationality. The treatment was a total success. The girl can now tolerate the proximity of birds and enjoys eating chicken. She is even developing an interest in ornithology.

To the layman there seems to be considerable overlap between hypnosis and other mental or 'mind control' techniques. At its simplest, hypnosis leads to relaxation, and most relaxation techniques, particularly Autogenic Training and Meditation, depend to some extent on self-hypnosis. Only comparatively recently have researchers concluded that the common therapeutic factor in all mental therapies is an improved ability to relax the mind and the body. Nowhere is this better illustrated than in the now accepted relationship between hypnotherapy, relaxation techniques and biofeedback.

99

Biofeedback

Biofeedback began as a laboratory technique in the early sixties and there it has mostly remained. This does not mean, because biofeedback has not had wide therapeutic application, that the considerable research effort into the technique has come to naught. The spin-off from biofeedback research during the past fifteen or so years is to some extent responsible for the now generally accepted notion that relaxation is an essential pre-condition of all healing therapies.

Biofeedback is a technique which provides a person with information about his internal organs. We all practise what might be called 'natural feedback'. For example, if you attempt to lift a heavy suitcase and find that you cannot raise it more than a few inches, your brain and the muscles of your arm engage in 'feedback'. The brain tells the muscle (and vice versa) that either it isn't up to the job of lifting the suitcase or that it should employ more muscle effort; this feedback is augmented and confirmed by information passing between the eyes and the brain.

Rational man has always believed that he could command the functions of his own body. He can walk, sing, smile, talk, laugh, lift, bend, stretch and perform a host of variants of those basic abilities. But at the same time he has had to accept that the activities of his internal organs – the nervous and digestive systems, the heart and so on – were automatic functions and completely beyond his control while awake or sleeping. To any researcher interested in finding out more about how the mind worked this almost primitive limitation on man's ability to control the functions of his own body was unacceptable. Biofeedback research began as an exercise to prove that man could indeed learn to control the apparently involuntary systems of the body. Biofeedback researchers in the United States therefore decided to confine their investigations to three areas of involuntary human activity which were thought to be proof against conscious control: the brain, heart rate and blood pressure. Although it was known that some Indian swamis and yogis could lower their heart and breathing rates to astonishing levels – but only after years of practice – it was soon realised that the mystical element inherent in such feats was

100

inappropriate to Western people.

Until research proves otherwise, we must assume, as most experimental psychologists still do, that we have in effect two brains – one on the left side of the head the other on the right. They are believed to be at once independent, with differing functions, yet interdependent. Creative activity is normally controlled by the right hemisphere; this side of the brain helps us respond one way or the other to music and pictures, to like or dislike people and things. The left hemisphere is the dominant side and controls and directs our verbal activities; the left side of the brain brings, if you like, order into chaos and makes us rational, objective human beings.*

It's been known for nearly sixty years that the brain is in a continual state of electrical activity. This activity varies with the demands made on the brain. Four differing patterns of electrical rhythms or 'brain waves' have been identified and these can be monitored by an electroencephalograph (EEG). The subject is connected through electrodes attached to the scalp to the EEG which amplifies the brain waves and records their fluctuations by moving pens on graph paper. The four rhythms or waves are identified as *alpha, beta, theta* and *delta*.

Alpha waves occur when we are relaxed and content, our minds are unfocussed and not concentrating on any particular task. *Alpha* is the pleasurable wave.

Beta waves occur when the brain is concentrating. When the EEG indicates *beta* waves, the subject is 'plugged in', reacting strongly to surroundings and the myriad ideas passing through the brain.

Theta waves dominate the brain wave pattern when we are on the verge of sleep, or under hypnosis. Therefore, *Theta* waves

---

* Many of the assumptions concerning the brain are likely to be overturned during the present decade largely as a result of the pioneering work of Professor John Lorber of the University of Sheffield. Now that improved technology enables 'layer' scans to be taken of any part of the brain, Dr Lorber has discovered that the upper part of the cranium need not be fully occupied by 'grey matter' for a person to live a fully effective life. Professor Lorber relates that a coroner sympathised with the parents of a young man who had died suddenly. The autopsy indicated that he had only a rudimentary brain. The parents were upset by the coroner's assumption that their son had been mentally deficient. He had lived a full and active life until a few days before his death.

101

are also associated with the transcendental state of mind sought by meditators.

Delta waves are the invariable accompaniment to deep sleep; they are also found in damaged brains.

Examining brain wave patterns on an EEG can be a dismaying experience. It confirms our subjective knowledge that our brains are in chaos most of the time; order only returns, and then only for comparatively brief periods, when we instruct the brain to concentrate and calculate or formulate. That the two hemispheres can, and usually do, show differing brain wave patterns simultaneously is further evidence of the anarchic nature of the human brain.

The assumption in the early days of biofeedback research was that if a person could summon alpha waves at will then this ability could lead to the control, possibly the elimination, of stress and tension. During the sixties – the days of flower power, the Beatles, the Maharishi and Transcendental Meditation (TM) – biofeedback was enthusiastically adopted by those who saw it as yet another method of reaching what was seen as some kind of psychological Nirvana – an altered state of consciousness. However, it is now generally accepted that there is little value in regarding the achievement of an 'alpha state', pleasurable though it might be, as a goal in itself.

Professor Aubrey Yates of the University of Western Australia and author of the standard account of biofeedback, regrets that 'science became entangled with philosophy in this way'. He believes that the most significant application of brain wave research will be in the treatment of epilepsy. Research shows a clear connection between electrical activity of the brain and epileptic fits. If, says Professor Yates, an epileptic could be taught through biofeedback to increase the alpha activity then it seems probable that the frequency of epileptic attacks could be reduced.

One of the leading biofeedback researchers in Britain is Professor Jasper Brener of the University of Hull. For some years he has been attempting to find out through a series of experiments how the heart rate can be voluntarily controlled. It's been known for some years that most people with minimal training can learn to vary the rate at which their hearts beat. What Professor Brener is trying to discover is how the control

102

system works. Does the heart rate go up or down in response to increasing or decreasing the general level of activity – that is becoming more tense or lapsing into relaxation – or can the heart rate be controlled independently of whether a person is tense or relaxed?

To do this, Professor Brener places a human 'guinea pig', usually a curious volunteer student, in a windowless, sound-proof booth. The subject is connected by electrodes to a sophisticated version of a lie detector. This measures not only heart rate, but also oxygen consumption, muscle activity or tension, general level of bodily activity, and skin conductance. Measurement of skin conductance makes use of the body's natural tendency to release minute amounts of perspiration when under stress – the principle of the lie detector.

Illuminated signs inside the booth indicate to the subject when he is to attempt to increase or decrease his heart rate. If the subject complies with the instruction to raise or lower his heart rate he is given aural and visual rewards: a tone is emitted and a meter indicates his success. Professor Brener's volunteers find it difficult to explain precisely how they control their heart rates. To bring it down, most subjects mentally 'switch off' and

This volunteer at Hull University has his bodily functions linked to recording devices. The hood over his head enables his breathing rate to be measured. He has trained himself to raise or lower his heart rate on a given signal.

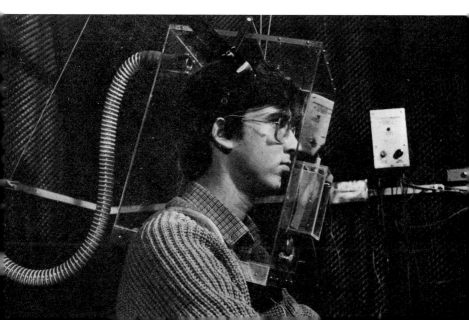

Professor Jasper Brener monitors the activity of internal organs during a biofeedback experiment.

attempt to relax in their own way: to raise it, they induce fear or terror simply by imagining a frightening scene or experience. Other people say they do it by thinking of people they like or dislike.

Very interesting, you say, but of what possible relevance is it to, for example, controlling heart disease? Biofeedback has not fulfilled the high hopes held out for it when research began in the early sixties. It is not a specific treatment for heart conditions. The most that can be claimed for the method is that it can help to lower the heart rate. This we know provides a general defence against stress-related complaints, but the question thrown up by the research still has not been answered: is the heart rate lowered as a result of the biofeedback or because of the relaxation it induces?

Dr Andrew Steptoe, of St George's Hospital Medical School, London, uses biofeedback to treat patients with hypertension (high blood pressure). He has had some success, but he is uncertain whether it is due to biofeedback or improved relaxation because, with his encouragement, most of his patients are undergoing biofeedback and relaxation training concurrently.

Dr Steptoe believes that biofeedback training is most effec-

104

tive when it is applied under conditions which approximate to those likely to be experienced by the patient in everyday life. He therefore includes a mildly stressful experience as part of the treatment; the patient is required to lower his blood pressure while at the same time doing simple mental arithmetic.

The patient sits alone in a comfortable chair in front of a television screen, connected by electrodes to equipment which gives a continuous read-out of pulse rate and blood pressure. An electronically generated horizontal line in the middle of the screen, representing the patient's blood pressure, is divided by a shorter vertical line. During the treatment session the patient receives continuous feedback from the television screen of his ability to control his blood pressure. If the vertical line goes above the horizontal line the blood pressure is rising, but if it goes below this indicates to the patient that he is being successful in his attempt to lower his blood pressure.

Dr Steptoe concedes that hypertensive patients might record reduced blood pressure as a result of meditation or a relaxation technique which would make all the sophisticated hardware of the biofeedback laboratory unnecessary. However, it seems that the value of biofeedback lies in the information it provides. Feedback is not available to a patient who attempts to relax or meditate. He may subjectively believe that by relaxing or meditating he is controlling his blood pressure, but he lacks the concrete proof provided by biofeedback. It may be, Dr Steptoe tentatively suggests, that biofeedback acts through unconscious mechanisms rather like a suggestion implanted under hypnosis. Perhaps its value lies in psychological conditioning. Biofeedback certainly gives the patient valuable self-knowledge and the confidence, born of the proven ability to control invisible physical functions, to continue the experiment in daily life.

Most patients who have been given biofeedback training find the experience so enjoyable that they are reluctant to end the treatment. Having had their eyes opened to the realisation that they are carrying around unseen equipment performing unfathomable but controllable functions, patients often seek self-training methods to enable them to build on the improvement resulting from biofeedback, or at least to recreate the sense of well-being it induced. Biofeedback machines are available for home treatment, but the purchase of one may persuade its owner to continue using it long after it should have proved unnecessary. After all, the purpose of the treatment is to help the patient break free of dependence upon equipment, to rely on his own ability to control internal functions.

Biofeedback specialists often advise their patients, particularly those with hypertension, to help maintain control of their blood pressure through non-mystical meditation or relaxation. One of the most effective relaxation techniques is Autogenic Training.

Autogenic Training

Autogenic Training was developed in the 1920s by a German psychiatrist J. H. Schultz, who practised hypnotherapy. Schultz noticed that his patients almost invariably reported feelings of heaviness and warmth in their limbs during hypnosis. He decided to find out whether heaviness and warmth could be induced by the patient independently of the hypnotherapist, and in a wakeful state. It soon became clear that a majority of patients could induce warmth and heaviness in their limbs simply by giving silent instructions to their arms or legs to become warm or heavy. Schultz announced his unbelievably simple method of relaxation in 1932, and although it has been widely practised in parts of Europe and in America it has only comparatively recently become available in Britain. Teaching in the method is available at the Centre for Autogenic Training formed in London in 1978, but it is possible to master the basic technique on your own.

Autogenic Training relies on systematically talking your arms and legs into a state of relaxation by first inducing heaviness, then warmth. Many people find it convenient to practise while lying in bed, prior to sleep; often sleep intervenes before the exercises are complete.

So, lying on your back in bed, arms to the side, legs a few inches apart, repeat the following formula silently to yourself without moving your lips; in other words, 'think' the formula. If you are left-handed begin with the left arm. Don't try too hard. Let it happen.

Heaviness

My right arm is heavy	(repeat three times)
My left arm is heavy	(repeat three times)
Both arms are heavy	(repeat three times)
My right leg is heavy	(repeat three times)
My left leg is heavy	(repeat three times)
Both legs are heavy	(repeat three times)
My arms and legs are heavy	(repeat three times)

Warmth

My right arm is warm	(repeat three times)
My left arm is warm	(repeat three times)
Both arms are warm	(repeat three times)
My right leg is warm	(repeat three times)
My left leg is warm	(repeat three times)
Both legs are warm	(repeat three times)
My arms and legs are warm	(repeat three times)

If you find that your concentration strays from the limb you are addressing, don't try and will yourself to concentrate. Calmly repeat the instruction to yourself and continue.

Each session should take about 6–7 minutes and should be practised twice a day – more if you have the time. Some people manage to fit in their autogenic training sessions while sitting on buses and trains.

After several weeks regular practice it should be possible to induce warmth or heaviness from the first instruction. You may find that warmth comes to the limbs during the heaviness exercises. Treat it as a bonus. All it means is that you've conditioned your mind and your body to expect it.

It's advisable to have qualified instruction for more advanced exercises or, at least, to read one of the recommended books in the reference section.

A word of warning. At the end of a session of Autogenic Training – unless you want to go to sleep – make sure that you are fully alert. You can do this by opening your eyes and clenching both fists. Then move your arms and legs. Finally, take a deep breath, yawn, and stretch.

Meditation

Largely as a result of the Beatles' association with the Maharishi Mahesh Yogi, his system of meditation known as Transcendental Meditation (TM) received such widespread publicity that many people must have thought that meditation began with the Maharishi. TM seemed to be semi-religious, probably because of the considerable impact of the Maharishi as a 'holy man' and the necessity of going through a curious initiation ceremony before a 'mantra' or 'keyword' could be imparted. The Maharishi undoubtedly revived meditation, but TM differs little from age-old methods of meditation which have formed a part of many religions.

Whatever its origins, meditation is now firmly established as a beneficial method of mind control. 'Mind control' has sinister connotations, but in this context it means attempting to achieve a 'blank mind', akin to the Zen or Yogic ideal, for a period of ten to twenty minutes. Like the basic exercises of Autogenic Training, meditation can be self-taught.

The effects of TM are undoubtedly beneficial as numerous medical assessments have indicated. TM has been shown to reduce heart rate and blood pressure, apart from inducing an overall reduction of tension. However, a research team at Harvard University led by Dr Herbert Benson discovered that the same results could be obtained if the mantra, of vital mystical significance to the Maharishi and his followers, were replaced by a simple word. Dr Benson tested a number of volunteers and asked them to meditate using a technique similar to TM, but with the mantra replaced by the word 'one'. The medical results were almost identical. Dr Benson made no great claims for this method of non-mystical meditation, the 'relaxation response' as he called it. He simply examined the ancient art of meditation and adapted it to modern conditions and requirements.

The Relaxation Response

   1 Sit quietly in a comfortable position with eyes closed.
   2 Deeply relax all your muscles, beginning at your feet and progressing up to your face. Keep them relaxed.

108

You might like to use the autogenic method of relaxation before starting meditation.

3 Breathe through the nose, easily and naturally. Become aware of your breathing. As you breathe out, say the word, 'ONE' silently to yourself.

4 Continue for 10–20 minutes. You may open your eyes to check the time, but do not use an alarm clock. When you finish, sit quietly for several minutes, at first with your eyes closed. Then sit for a few minutes with your eyes open before standing up.

At first you will find it difficult to shut out all thoughts, but don't grit your teeth and become determined to achieve a blank mind. This will have the opposite effect. Try to become passive and receptive to the idea of relaxation. Concentrate on 'ONE'. Two sessions daily are recommended, but not within two hours after a meal because you will find your conscious intentions are in a losing combat with your digestive process.

NATHANIEL GREATRAKES, *Esq.*
a Native of Waterford County,
———— IRELAND. ————

& most Remarkable *for* Curing many Disorders *by the* Stroke *or*
Touch *of his Hand only.*

Pub. by Alex. Hogg, 16, Paternoster-row, March 1 1805.

Eighteenth-century Irish hand healer, Nathaniel Greatrakes.

Healing

Healing is a matter of time, but it is sometimes a matter of opportunity.

Hippocrates

The woman came into the healer's room. She was hot, flustered and irritated. She was angry at being delayed by London traffic and for allowing herself to be persuaded to consult a healer. She did not believe in healing and almost the first words she spoke to the healer were, 'I'm sure it won't work'. The healer, a young man in his twenties, unprovoked by the woman's aggressive demeanour, responded courteously. After several years successful healing he has become familiar with patients who attempt to cloak their hopes in disbelief.

'It won't work because I don't believe in it,' the woman remarked. 'And I'm not religious.' The healer calmly replied that neither belief in healing nor religious faith were necessary for healing to occur although, he suggested, the healing process might be helped if the woman could abandon her antagonism during the healing session.

In response to the healer's quiet enquiries the woman described her complaint. For over two years she had suffered from pains in her hips. The condition was worsening and she feared that she was developing a serious disease like multiple sclerosis or rheumatoid arthritis. Orthodox treatment, while controlling the pain with various drugs, had failed to find and eliminate the cause.

The healer stood behind the woman and laid his hands gently on her shoulders and closed his eyes. He remained in this position for several minutes and then knelt down and placed his hands on the woman's left knee. After several minutes he moved his hands to the right knee. His eyes were closed. Neither healer nor patient spoke. Deftly but calmly the healer moved to the site of the pains. He cupped the woman's left hip

111

joint in his hands. After a few minutes she seemed to be suffering some discomfort. 'I'm afraid the pain's getting worse,' she said. The healer smiled briefly, but unmistakably with satisfaction, and moved to the other hip.

Then a look of astonishment mixed with delight and imminent tears crossed the woman's face. 'It's gone,' she said. 'The pain's gone in the other hip. This one's getting very hot. And I can feel a sort of tingling coming from your hands.' The treatment continued in silence for a few more minutes. Then the healer asked the woman to stand up. 'It's amazing,' she said. 'Standing up like this is when it usually hurts most, but it doesn't hurt at all now. I can't believe it.' Several months later she was still free of pain.

Healing in Britain has more practitioners and more patients than all other alternative therapies combined. About 20,000 full or part-time healers practise the ancient art of healing

(a) Henri IV of France touching the sick. It was widely accepted that kings had divine healing powers.
(b) A regular healing service in the crypt of Coventry Cathedral.

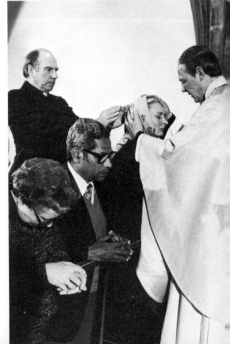

sickness by the laying on of hands. To the rest of the Western world Britain is regarded as the spiritual home of healing. Here healers enjoy an envied status and freedom. In most European countries healing is illegal; in some American states healers are tolerated but may not touch their patients. By contrast the three thousand-odd members of the National Federation of Spiritual Healers are permitted to work in hospitals and doctors can refer patients to healers. But for all that, healing to many people is slightly distasteful, lumped together with crystal gazing and palmistry and practised by mildly sinister ladies in bombazine.

Healing and Religion

For decades healing has been inextricably linked either with spiritualism or religious belief, but as alternative medicine becomes more widely accepted, there is a discernible reluctance by many healers to be known as 'faith' or 'spiritual' healers; they would prefer to be regarded simply as healers. Confusion remains, but is easily dispersed if we understand that spiritualism offers a channel of communication with the dead through a medium who acts as an intermediary. A 'spiritual healer' is also regarded as a medium, the representative of a 'spirit doctor' or healer who conveys healing power to the living sick. A 'spiritual healer' would typically not deny a religious belief, but a 'faith healer' places most emphasis on belief in God as the fount of all healing and may or may not subscribe to spiritualism. Harry Edwards, probably the most successful British healer during this century, was both a spiritual and faith healer. But whatever name they choose to adopt, healers heal primarily by the laying on of hands.

Most of us can recall the sense of comfort we derived as children from physical contact – kiss, touch or hug – with an affectionate adult. Our tears dried up, the graze or the bump on the head seemed to become less painful because of the 'hug to make it better'. It's well known that children deprived of physical contact during childhood are more likely to suffer disturbed psychological behaviour as adults.

A recent American research project has noted the importance of touch even in everyday transactions. The research

113

revealed that, if, when you pay for goods in a shop, you unconsciously touch the hand of the shop assistant you will almost certainly be rewarded with a smile or perhaps an unexpected willingness to make certain that the purchase is entirely satisfactory. If no physical contact takes place this response is less common. While such information should not be taken as an encouragement to stroke the hands of shop assistants, it does provide further evidence that we in the twentieth century world are perhaps denying ourselves access to a valuable 'life support system'.

Further evidence attesting the therapeutic value of the laying on of hands comes from research conducted by Dolores Krieger, Professor of Nursing at New York University. Encouraged by the results she herself obtained, Professor Krieger trains nurses to apply hand healing in appropriate cases. The results are impressive. Patients tended by 'nurse-healers' recover more quickly and the quality of their blood is measurably improved.

Of all the leading alternative therapies, healing is the most elusive. It repels close examination because even its leading exponents find it difficult, if not impossible, to describe what they are doing when they heal. The sensation of warmth (occasionally coldness or tingling) reported by patients during healing provides circumstantial evidence that something more than physical contact between the healer and the patient is occurring, but it does not contribute much to our understanding of the healing power. Depending on their particular persuasion, healers talk of energy fields, of a divine healing power which is about us all the time; they are the channel or conduit through which it is imparted to those who need it. Healers deny that they do the healing. The healing power emanates from the source of the healing, whatever it is, and the patient, because of his own desire to regain health, becomes attuned to it and then heals himself. Certainly no healer would claim that he alone is the creator of his healing power.

So what is happening between healer and patient? Bruce Macmanaway, a practising healer for over forty years, thinks that some form of energy flows through and is 'conducted or transformed' into the patient. 'If I am right,' he says, 'this suggests that there is a higher intelligence directing the energy

114

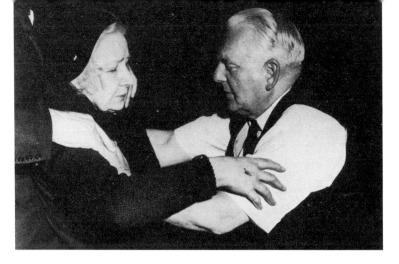

The late Harry Edwards was probably the most successful British healer of this century.

because I'm often unaware of the patient's real problem yet they get better. The sheer strength of the energy is quite phenomenal yet I don't have to summon it. I only have to place my hand on or even near a patient for the energy to be felt.' Most of Bruce Macmanaway's patients experience intense heat coming from his hands. The sensation is similar to a hot water bottle in a cover being placed on the skin. Other patients describe the opposite sensation – a penetrating coldness like a cold draught playing on the area or a tingling similar to pins and needles. Occasionally patients say that one hand is hot and the other cold although the healer is quite unaware of any sensation himself.

Bruce Macmanaway discovered his gift for healing when in the Army during the war. He found that he could help wounded men simply by putting his hands on them. 'They told me pain disappeared and I could see for myself that often bleeding stopped and there was no subsequent septicaemia although we had no sterile dressings.' Throughout his service career he regularly healed soldiers of aches, pains and strains. He now practises mostly in Scotland where he also teaches healing, but he sees patients in London as well.

Unlike most healers, Bruce Macmanaway uses a pendulum to help him make an initial diagnosis. It is a strange sight: a large man with a personality to match holding a small perspex

115

The Medicine Men

pendulum on a chain in front of the patient and watching its movements intently as it 'responds' to mostly unspoken questions. It seems unnecessary, almost theatrical, and patients almost always find it amusing, but they accept it because for most of them all other treatment has failed. For Bruce Macmanaway the pendulum is a simple but indispensable diagnostic aid. 'The pendulum will do nothing for me in its own right. It is more an amplifier of a signal which is already in the patient.'

The pendulum can only answer concise, unambiguous questions about the patient's condition. It 'answers' by oscillating – clockwise means 'yes' and anti-clockwise means 'no'; if the pendulum moves in a straight line it's puzzled and is saying the equivalent of 'don't know'. There are other possible oscillations like a clockwise or anti-clockwise ellipse which usually indicates confusion or that the question is poorly expressed or unanswerable.*

Many of the questions concern the condition of the back because Bruce Macmanaway believes many ailments are caused by, or aggravated by, minute dislocations of the spine.

Like most healers Bruce Macmanaway makes few claims for his abilities, invariably stressing that he is only a channel for the healing energy. He points out that most of his patients are also receiving medical treatment. He tentatively believes that well over half the people who come to his healing centre in Fife are helped in some way, 'but whether it is that we have tipped the scale so they respond to the doctor's treatment or whether we've done something really significant by ourselves really doesn't matter – the great thing is that the patient does improve.'

It is a source of great amusement to healers that until the repeal of the Witchcraft Act in 1952 they could have been prosecuted as witches! Anyone bearing less resemblance to a witch than Bruce Macmanaway cannot be imagined. He thinks that healers are tolerated in Britain because of our *laissez faire* attitude to anyone who is not causing harm and may be doing good. Long before the General Medical Council permitted doctors to refer patients to non-medical practitioners he was

* Further information about the use of the pendulum will be found in the chapter on radiesthesia and radionics, p. 129.

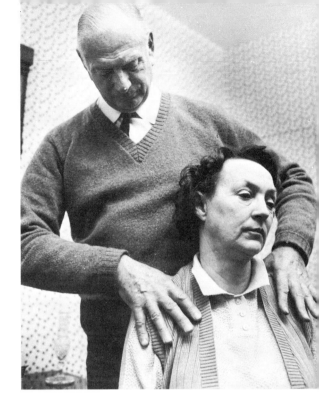

Bruce Macmanaway runs training courses for healers in Scotland and regularly holds healing sessions in London.

treating not only doctors' patients, but also doctors themselves. Every year, either in Scotland or in various parts of Europe, he trains doctors in the art of healing.

From the start of his career, a London general practitioner, Dr Michael Gormley, made no secret of his interest in natural medicine. He regularly refers patients to osteopaths, chiropractors, acupuncturists and healers. He does it solely in the interests of the patient and feels no sense of failure if, say, an osteopath is successful where orthodox medicine has failed. 'My interest in natural medicine,' he says, 'is becoming stronger and stronger as I realise that many of the treatments are relatively safer and without the side-effects we associate with much of orthodox medicine. I hope in time my colleagues will lose some of their prejudices against natural therapies because they and the patients can only benefit.'

A different route to gaining acceptance for healing within the medical profession has been taken by Dr Una Kroll, a GP in South London. In her capacity as a Deaconess of the Church of

117

England she has spoken and preached frequently on the lapsed association between religious faith and healing. Dr Kroll thinks the Church establishment is mistaken in continuing to ignore the Christian message, 'Go thou and heal the sick'. She would like to see a much closer association between local ministers and doctors. It would not of course suit everyone, she says, but in her practice she suggests healing in a religious context if it seems appropriate.

Because we live in an essentially materialist world, successful scientific experiments which tend to prove the subjective claims of unorthodox therapies are immensely encouraging to the world of alternative medicine. Healers know, and their patients know, that they can effect remarkable cures. But they cannot prove it, in the sense that Drug X can be proved to lower blood pressure or Drug Y to induce sleep. Healers have survived ridicule and disbelief for centuries, but some modern healers feel that they have been outsiders for long enough. Many of them want nothing less than a scientific stamp of approval. During the early seventies paranormal researchers thought that at last a way had been found of proving psychic phenomena, particularly healing, and despatching the gibes of the 'all in the mind' camp. It was at first confidently claimed that no scientist could ignore the evidence provided by Kirlian photography.

Kirlian photography – named after the Russian couple who discovered and developed it – is a method of photographing (perhaps, more correctly, of registering or recording) the aura or corona which, psychics claim, surrounds all living matter. A Kirlian machine is not a camera, although it utilises ordinary photographic paper to produce images. It consists of a flat, insulated metal plate on top of a small box which conceals a high voltage, high-frequency electrical coil. A sheet of photographic paper is placed on the machine and the object to be tested is brought into contact with it. The current is passed through the plate, the paper, and the object for a few seconds. Provided the object is emitting its own energy its interaction or collision with the electrical current will produce 'sparks' which are recorded on the paper.

Two leading British scientists who are interested in the paranormal, Professor John Taylor and Professor John Hasted of

118

Kirlian photographs of the hands of a patient immediately before
and after healing. Kirlian researchers claim the indistinct *'before'*
photograph (above) shows the patient is lacking energy. The
clearer *'after'* photograph (below) is said to represent the 'healed'
patient's new higher energy level.

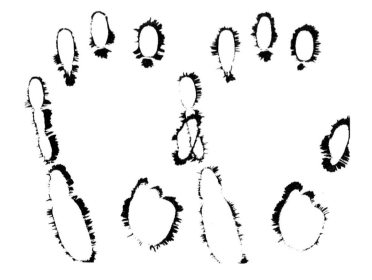

the University of London, are critical of the technique of Kirlian photography. 'For a scientific method it has too many uncontrollable variables,' says Professor Hasted. Professor Taylor claims that results are affected at random by the varying pressure of the hand or the finger on the recording plate, the amount of moisture in the skin, even the angle of the finger on the plate. Professor Taylor has unequivocally stated that 'from my own and other scientists' tests on the process, Kirlian photography is irrelevant to paranormal investigations'.

Scientists have avoided healing as a suitable subject of inquiry possibly because they realise that the answer does not lie in the area in which they feel most comfortable – the world of quantifiable phenomena and facts and statements susceptible to cast-iron proof. But change is in the air and some British scientists are beginning to come out into the open and declare an interest in supernatural occurrences.

Professor John Hasted of the department of physics at Birkbeck College, University of London, together with several colleagues conducted laboratory tests on the healing ability of the young English healer Matthew Manning. In one experiment Matthew gave 'healing' to mould spore and achieved a significant reduction in its rate of growth.

Healing had a less spectacular effect on the activity of an enzyme known as monoamine oxidase, or MAO, a deficiency of which is thought to cause migraine. The biochemical function of MAO, like all enzymes, is to make changes in the body's metabolism. The experimenters isolated MAO from human blood and gave a sample in two test tubes to Matthew Manning; another sample was given to a non-healer and the third was left in another room at the same temperature.

The samples in a glass beaker were placed in front of Matthew Manning and the non-healer for several minutes. The results were encouraging but inconsistent. The second and third samples were almost unchanged, but the activity of the MAO in Matthew's test tube was found to have either increased or decreased considerably indicating that Matthew was responsible.

Because of the fluctuating results Professor Hasted is cautious in making large claims for the significance of this research: 'What is the use of a car which goes backwards or forwards but you can't tell which direction it's going in?' Matthew's ability to heal patients had been observed and was not in question, but Professor Hasted thinks it significant that his power has been shown to affect matter in test tubes surrounded by all the paraphernalia of modern science. 'There is something there,' he says. 'We don't know what it is yet, but Matthew makes strange unpredictable things happen. They deserve further study to find out the nature of this power.'

In common with most healers, Matthew accepts that whatever powers he has are not his to exploit unduly for his own personal gain. From the mid-seventies onwards he took part in numerous scientific experiments in Canada, the United States, Holland, Sweden, Germany and Britain. In America he satisfied researchers at the Mind Science Foundation in Texas that paranormal influences were operating when he demonstrated his ability to extend the life of red blood cells when placed in a hostile environment. The cells were placed in a weak saline solution which would normally kill them within five minutes. Matthew applied 'healing' which extended the life of the cells by about twelve minutes. In other experiments at the Mind Science Foundation, Matthew was able to make a gerbil run faster on a treadmill or, in the cautious words of the report, 'to induce, mentally and at a distance, an increase in the locomotor behaviour of a small rodent which reached a marginal level of significance'.

In an analysis of a period of two years' intense scientific

Matthew Manning attempts to affect the activity of the human enzyme, MAO, in the test tube.

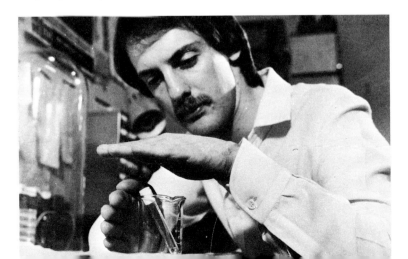

experimentation Matthew found that he was considerably more successful when working with humans or biological specimens than with electronic hardware. It also became apparent that his results were often influenced by his level of rapport with the scientist. Poor rapport or an inexperienced researcher nearly always resulted in failure of the experiment. This lends support to the assertion made by most healers that an amenable subject can assist the healing process.

Although Matthew Manning gives public demonstrations of healing in Britain and Europe, he prefers treating individual patients at his Midlands clinic. An appointment lasts about twenty minutes to half an hour. He usually begins with a brief diagnostic interview. 'I always ask the patient first what is wrong. It saves time and sometimes it tells me something about the person which is helpful.' Occasionally he corrects a medical mis-diagnosis simply by interpreting the emanations coming from the patient. He advised one patient who had been told he had cancer of the bladder to have a fresh diagnosis because he was not 'picking up' the cancer while healing. The second doctor confirmed Matthew's intuitive belief that the man did not have cancer. 'I try to attune myself to the patient,' he says. 'I mentally see the different problems the person is suffering from.'

Matthew shares the belief of most healers that negative thoughts – repressed feelings of anger, guilt, hostility – are often responsible for illness. At public demonstrations and lectures about healing he demonstrates the effect such negative thinking has on our bodies. Try it yourself:

Have someone stand in front of you, back towards you, right arm extended to the side at shoulder height; for a left-handed person begin with the left arm. Ask the person to bring to mind some unpleasant thought – sadness, or anger about a person or an experience. The subject should concentrate on the thought while you press down with one hand placed in the middle of the outstretched arm. Even strong men will not be able to resist the pressure of your hand and you will find that you can force it down without difficulty. Now try the other arm. Ask the subject to extend the left arm while concentrating on some pleasant thought – an enjoyable experience or a much-loved person. Apply similar pressure to the mid-point of the arm as before. You will find that most people are able to call up unimagined resources of strength and can resist the pressure. Matthew gives this as a simple example of the tenet that negative thoughts weaken while positive thoughts strengthen. We know this instinctively, but there is scientific evidence of its truth. Russian researchers have discovered that the supply of white blood cells – the body's first line of defence against illness – is increased by positive emotions while negative thoughts decrease the body's ability to attack and destroy invading organisms.

The power of positive thought to overcome problems and difficulties and to heal sickness characterises the approach to healing of another leading British healer, Tom Johanson. Tom Johanson runs the Spiritualist Association of Great Britain – claimed to be the largest organisation of its kind in the world – from a large house in London's Belgrave Square. On most mornings there is a cluster of people waiting on the pavement for the doors to open. Thoughout the day – it's open seven days a week – many will visit or telephone seeking help and advice, succour, spiritual guidance or healing. There is a sprinkling of people who regard the SAGB as a club and visit it every day, finding, or at least seeking, whatever it is they need in the library, the bookshop, the chapel or the cafeteria; and there are those who just enjoy being there.

The Association's healing clinic is open to anyone without appointment. Several healers are on duty every day in the healing cubicles at the top of the building attempting to cure illnesses that have failed to respond to orthodox treatment. The visitors are mostly older people, many of them visibly ailing or disabled who, as a last resort, are handing themselves over to a stranger whom they believe has healing in his or her hands.

Tom Johanson has administered the SAGB since 1968 but he is a reluctant bureaucrat and sees himself first and foremost as a healer. Like many others he took to healing because he was told he was a natural healer. For many years he resisted 'the call' to full-time healing because he had serious doubts about his healing ability. When he did eventually commit himself he felt that his whole life had been a preparation for this task. Tom Johanson believes that humility and compassion characterise all healers. 'Compassion,' he says, 'is the highest form of prayer, but it also means being able to "tune in" to the suffering of others. Healers are used as healing agents, but the gift lies in

123

their compassion. There can be no healing without compassion.'

For Sussex healer Phil Edwardes it is by no means uncommon to be approached by patients with the full approval of a local general practitioner. Dr Priscilla Noble-Matthews believes that orthodox medicine is in danger of losing its way through the maze of chemical drugs. 'Our concern as doctors,' she says, should be to 'cure sometimes, alleviate often, and comfort always, but most of us fall far short of that ideal.' She believes that what a patient needs most is time; time to express subjective feelings about his state of health and time to be listened to.

Dr Noble-Matthews has formed a close link with Phil Edwardes in order to study what happens to his patients over a period of five years. She intends to interview all of his patients before and after healing and will eventually produce what she believes will be the first properly conducted medical assessment of a healer and his patients.

For his part, Phil Edwardes is co-operating fully with Dr Noble-Matthews because his own experience as a healer shows clearly that those patients whom orthodox medicine has more or less abandoned as incurable can be helped. He hopes that the survey will persuade doctors that healing can be an effective therapy. A former garage owner, he discovered his healing ability by chance when he was with a group of friends, one of whom, a woman, had extreme soreness due to an allergy on her back. For some reason which he cannot explain, he felt impelled to offer help. He placed his hands on the woman's back. She said that almost immediately she felt great heat from his hands. After continuing the treatment for several minutes he removed his hands, feeling, he recalls, slightly foolish. The woman, however, claimed that her recovery started from the moment that treatment began.

Phil Edwardes now practises as a healer full-time at his cottage in Sussex. Throughout the week there is a steady stream of patients. Most come by appointment and although he discourages the chance caller he will always offer treatment. He works in his small consulting room to a background of muted classical music. He starts each session with a friendly enquiry about the nature of the complaint and what changes, if any,

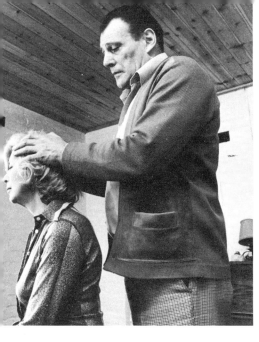

Ex-garage owner, Phil Edwardes, heals patients in his Sussex healing centre.

there have been since the last healing. For a minute or two he sits behind the patient with his eyes closed until his hands begin to shake. He says that the channel between what he calls 'the Guv'nor' and himself and the patient is always open, but it is still necessary for him to be sure the healing energy is there before concentrating it on the patient. With his hands still shaking he stands up and places them gently at the sides of the patient's head. He remains in this position for several minutes before moving to the afflicted part of the body. The consultation ends after about ten to fifteen minutes with a brief inquiry about the effects of the healing, conducted in a model bedside manner. Phil Edwardes' healing technique and his comforting personality have a calming effect and most patients remark that for the period of the healing they experience deep calm or relaxation.

Phil Edwardes is unwilling to make a guess at his success rate. Like all healers, he can never be sure, if after one session a patient does not return, whether or not he has been successful. One of his most interesting cases was a young girl who was accidentally shot in the knee by a twelve-bore shotgun at a range of six feet. Amputation or an operation to render the leg rigid were considered, but the girl held out against surgery

125

although she was in constant severe pain. Within seconds of the treatment starting the girl burst into tears because for the first time for months she became free of pain. Weekly treatment continued for several months and 'before and after' x-ray pictures (below) show that new bone had been encouraged to grow on the knee joint. Although the girl has a slightly mis-shapen knee she is able to run, dance, ride a horse or a bicycle, and is free of pain.

A young married woman who suffered severe spinal damage after falling in a river and landing on a sharp rock came to see Phil Edwardes. She was in great pain and had been told by surgeons that there was nothing that could be done and that she would have to live with her disability. After ten months of regular healing the woman was totally cured and is able to live a normal pain-free life.

Phil Edwardes is regularly presented with all kinds of con-ditions, but he has had particular success with back problems. It gives him much personal satisfaction when he is able to relieve pain, particularly in cancer patients, or to make the

X-rays of the knee joint before (left) and after healing show shot pellets still lodged in the leg. The arrow indicates where significant new bone growth has occurred. Doctors still express surprise that she is not in any pain. Exercise now produces no discomfort in the knee joint (opposite page).

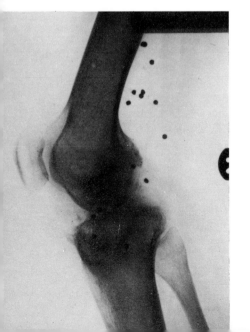
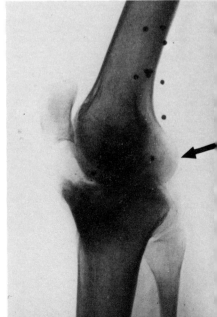

experience of approaching death more bearable. One man suffering from cancer of the gullet was unable to swallow even a glass of water and was on a heavy dose of pain-killers before healing. After healing, the pain faded enough to render painkillers unnecessary. For the last three weeks of his life he was also able to eat and drink normally. He was able to die without pain and with dignity.

Finding a Healer

Finding a healer is not difficult. Any of the healing organisations listed at the back of the book will either recommend a healer or give advice about their own healing services. The quality of healers is, of course, variable. If you find your chosen healer has had no effect on your complaint it is always worth trying another because healing depends in some measure on the rapport that exists between healer and patient. Some healers, knowing that healing does not originate in themselves, forgo all payment; others seek a 'donation' according to the ability of the patient to pay. Another method, acceptable to most patients, is to charge for the time expended.

Radiesthesia and Radionics

Only a few diseases have their seat where they can be seen.
Hippocrates

If you approach a radiesthetist, or a radionics practitioner, you will be asked to cut off some of your hair, or prick yourself with a sterilised needle and let a drop of blood fall on to a piece of blotting paper. To a practitioner of radiesthesia or radionics, the hair or the blood is your 'witness'; it represents you as much as if you had presented yourself in person. From it the practitioner claims to be able to ascertain your present condition, the best treatment to administer, and often any future illnesses that your body contains, but has yet to manifest. This may sound far-fetched in comparison with most other alternative therapies, but radiesthesia and radionics have been practised long enough for their shortcomings to have been exposed.

Both radiethesia and its younger brother, radionics, are based on the theory that all matter in the world is both transmitting and receiving emanations. Radiesthesia is a method of diagnosing and treating illness through dowsing or divining. Radionics is similar to radiesthesia, but relies for diagnosis and treatment on instruments allied to telepathy or extra-sensory perception (ESP).

Radiesthesia

How curious it is that man can reach the moon, invent radar and computers yet sometimes cannot find the water main. Armed with nothing more than a forked hazel branch, a rod or a pendulum, even a coathanger or bare hands, the dowser methodically patrols the area thought to be the site of water mentally asking the dowsing instrument to confirm or deny its

129

presence. If water is present, the dowsing instrument will react by vibrating or being pulled downwards, sometimes so violently that it is wrenched out of the dowser's hands. When pressed to explain their ability, one that many people have been found to possess, dowsers tend to resort to phrases like 'natural sensitivity', 'sixth sense', 'mind over matter' and 'sensing vibrations'.

The terms dowsing and water divining are taken to be interchangeable, but dowsing can do more than find water mains and underground streams. Dowsers have helped builders find potentially dangerous mine workings, cables, pipes and drains; they are sometimes called in to help at archaeological digs and in the search for oil and gas. In Holland, the Dutch police, asked to find a missing person, often turn for help to a dowser who has had spectacular success. And during the Vietnam war dowsers were sometimes employed (successfully) by US Marines to locate Vietcong tunnels.

Primitive societies instinctively applied the dowsing facility to healing. Numerous anthropological studies in the earlier part of this century reported that a pendulum or divining rod was widely used in Africa and South America by medicine men who almost certainly practised their traditional methods in the unchanged form in which they had been handed down from generation to generation. In Europe the work of the tribal medicine man is performed by, among others, the hand healer and it may be that healing by the laying on of hands relies partly on dowsing. Many healers claim that during treatment they are drawn to the site of an illness even if the patient does not identify or locate it.

The connection between dowsing and medical diagnosis was made in the early years of this century when a French priest, the Abbé Alexis Mermet (1866–1937), made the first intuitive jump that would establish the medical application of the ancient art. Mermet knew that dowsers were not only able to locate water beneath the ground, but they could also distinguish its quality. The ability to 'sense' pure water from polluted water, Mermet reasoned, could surely be applied to identifying and locating the infected parts in an otherwise healthy body. Mermet made no great claims for his theories or his abilities, but simply stated that the analogy between the interior of the

(a) This early eighteenth-century dowser is unmasked by a priest and shown to be the devil with horns, cloven hoof and tail. The Church opposed any power which could be seen as a threat to its authority.
(b) Abbé Alexis Mermet (1866–1937) first linked dowsing to medicine.

human body and the subterranean world was too strong to be ignored. Within the body and under the surface of the earth there was an unseen, and at that time largely unknown, world each with its own intricate system of channels and lakes and passages.

The Abbé Mermet was one of the world's most successful dowsers. He achieved widespread fame in Europe, accompanied by a certain notoriety which sprang from his uncanny ability to find wanted or missing people. Working only with a photograph or an article recently worn or handled by the missing person and maps of the area where he or she had last been seen, Mermet held a pendulum over the map and silently asked questions designed to indicate the whereabouts of the missing person.

Mermet's most astonishing case occurred in Switzerland in 1934. When he was asked to find a small boy who had

131

disappeared, Mermet, working in his usual way with map and pendulum and a personal article, claimed that the boy had been snatched by an eagle and taken up into the mountains. Searchers eventually found the boy's body when the snows melted. It was clear that he could not have climbed the mountain because his shoes and clothes were unmarked; his body bore injuries consistent with having been attacked by an eagle.

Mermet's belief that dowsing could have a medical application was supported by his contemporary, the Abbé Alexis Bouly. Bouly is usually credited with christening medical dowsing with its cumbersome identity – *radiesthesie* or radiesthesia. As a result of the work of these pioneers, radiesthesia was enthusiastically practised in Europe – particularly in France, Germany and Italy – but it was not until the early thirties that it crossed the Channel.

It is impossible to apply scientific methods to support a theory of radiesthesia. The most accessible starting point is the common experience of extra-sensory perception (ESP). Many people are frightened or disturbed by ESP even in its most harmless manifestation. The frequently experienced 'I have been here before' feeling causes a shudder in some people while

Arthur Bailey, President of the British Society of Dowsers, locates an underground stream and unmarked mine shafts on a map using a pendulum.

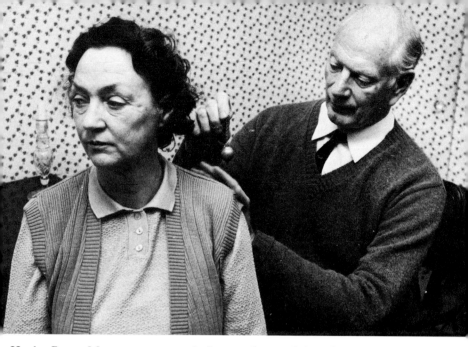

Healer Bruce Macmanaway regularly uses the pendulum for
diagnosis. He swings it close to the patient's body and mentally
asks it questions. By the direction of swing he deduces where the
patient's trouble lies.

others are excited by it. Voices in the mind, premonition, the
sensed presence of a benign or harmful being, the 'I wonder
what happened to X' kind of conversation which seems to
prompt a telephone call from X, are within the experience of
most people. If we can accept ESP at its simplest and least
frightening level, it is possible we are all in unconscious communication with each other. How otherwise could premonition
be received or conveyed? We all know that in families, or in
small groups of intimates, each member seems to be emitting
signals which convey thoughts and feelings to the others as
effectively as if they had been spoken. We are constantly radiat-
ing signals, but only people sensitive to our particular emanations will receive and respond to them.

Radiesthesia in practice   The Abbé Mermet practised
medical dowsing. He held a pendulum over the body of a

133

patient, and diagnosed the complaint; treatment he mostly left to the doctor. Some modern radiesthetists follow Mermet's method, but most use rules, charts and 'witnesses', as well as the pendulum. They also prescribe treatment, usually homoeopathic.

Before treatment can begin the patient will be asked to supply what radiesthetic practioners call a 'witness': a blood or hair sample or, occasionally, a photograph. Most patients who consult radiesthetists have a recognisable disease which, in most cases, has not responded to conventional treatment. Even if the practitioner knows that the patient is suffering from, say, migraine he will invariably do a 'vitality test'. The vitality test not only enables the practitioner to assess the extent of the pain, but it will also often indicate if the patient has any other illness. An experienced radiesthetist, like his counterpart in orthodox medicine, can often visually assess the overall health of the patient which he then confirms by using the pendulum.

An experienced radiesthetist, Vernon Wethered, uses a ruler calibrated to 100 cm to ascertain the general state of health of the patient. With the rule placed on an east-west axis the practitioner faces north with the patient's witness to his left, or in the west at point zero. The practitioner then holds his

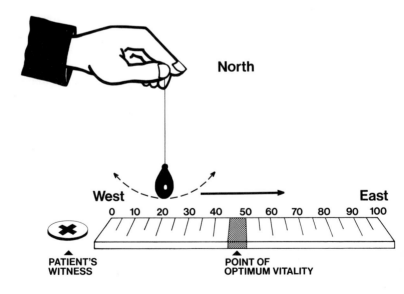

Pendulums come in many shapes, colours and sizes. Most practitioners have a favourite design which they claim gives them more accurate results.

pendulum over the rule and moves it slowly in an easterly direction. At some point along the rule the pendulum will, says Wethered, start to swing at right angles to the rule. If 45–50 cm is taken as the point of 'optimum vitality' – then any variation from that indicates by how much the patient falls short of first class health.

Having established that the patient's health is impaired, the practitioner next wants to find out what the patient is suffering from. Again, the practitioner will expect the pendulum to confirm what the patient is saying. If you are thinking that radiesthesia is something of a hit-or-miss affair, the next stage of treatment very much qualifies for that description. Radiesthetists might not disagree, but would suggest that the incidence of hits is higher than the misses.

What the radiesthetist seeks to do now is to find out what organ is affected and by what disease; he also wants to know how serious it is. Most radiesthetists in France and Britain use the system of disease and organ witnesses developed in the 1920s by a French engineer named Louis Turenne. Turenne proposed that the emanations given off by the blood of a diseased human should find some echo in those coming from a 'witness' representing the disease. He claimed that it was possible to impregnate an inert substance with the characteristics,

135

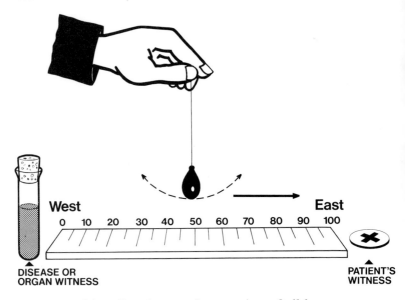

West   East

0 10 20 30 40 50 60 70 80 90 100

DISEASE OR ORGAN WITNESS   **PATIENT'S WITNESS**

represented by vibrations or frequencies, of all human organs and most diseases. He exposed small vials of the substance to human and animal organs and to a number of diseases.

To ascertain or confirm what disease the patient is suffering from, or what organ is affected, the practitioner places the rule or chart along an east-west axis. Facing north, with the patient's witness to his right or in the east and the organ or disease witness at the western end or to his left, the radiesthetist sets to work again with his pendulum. Holding the pendulum a few inches above the rule or chart the practitioner moves from left to right until it reacts, usually by oscillating across the rule. If the diagnosis provided by the disease witness is unclear the practitioner might carry out a further test by replacing it with an organ witness.

Having arrived at a satisfactory diagnosis, the radiesthetist usually selects, with the help of the pendulum, a homoeopathic remedy in a potency which he believes to be correct for the complaint. The pendulum, in answer to accurately worded, silent questions confirms or rejects the remedy or, possibly, suggests a higher or lower potency. For most practitioners the pendulum answers 'yes' by swinging clockwise; anti-clockwise means 'no' and the equivalent of 'don't know' is indicated by an uncertain oscillation which is neither clearly clockwise or anti-clockwise.

This may seem an extraordinary method of treating illness, but radiesthetists claim that they have had successes where orthodox medicine failed. If we adhere rigidly to the common currency of our time that medicine is science and has nothing whatever to do with unseen and unmeasurable forces, then we will undoubtedly rule radiesthesia out of court. If, however, we are able to make the jump, the jump that allows us partially to accept ESP, astrology or palmistry, then radiesthesia would not

A radionic analysis. The patient's hair sample is on the plate below the pendulum. As the practitioner's left hand touches diagrams representing the perfect condition of each organ, the pendulum 'tells' him how far the patient deviates from optimum health.

be a stranger in such a stable.

Radiesthesia is most buoyant in its country of origin. There are over a hundred radiesthetic practitioners in France where they are accorded recognition as a professional group by the Ministry of Labour and have their own union, the *Syndicat des Radiesthésistes*. In Britain radiesthesia is mostly practised in conjunction with homoeopathy, herbalism and acupuncture. It is most closely associated with radionics which has been described as 'instrumented radiesthesia'.

Radionics

Radionics arose from the chance discovery of an eminent American physician, Dr Albert Abrams. In the early years of this century Dr Abrams was examining a middle-aged man with cancer of the lip using standard orthodox techniques, including percussion. To percuss a patient, a doctor usually places the middle finger of one hand at various points on the body, usually the torso, and taps it with the tip of the middle finger of the other hand. In health, percussion produces a strong hollow-sounding, resonant note; a dull or muffled sound usually emanates only from a diseased body.

Dr Abrams would not have been expecting to find anything untoward because his patient had not complained of any internal disorder, but what he did discover was that while the man's abdomen generally gave off the clear note of health on percussion, there was one point which sounded muffled. Why Dr Abrams turned the patient to face in different directions is not known, but in doing so he found that the dull note could be picked up by percussion only when the patient faced west. Dr Abrams tested his observation on a number of patients suffering from different complaints. He percussed their abdomens and found that without exception he was able to locate a 'dull note spot' if the subjects were facing west. Dr Abrams next discovered that certain diseases and the dull note spots on the abdomen could be correlated. Thus, a dull note coming from a point below the navel was associated with tuberculosis; the tell-tale dull note coming from the left of the abdomen meant malaria.

138

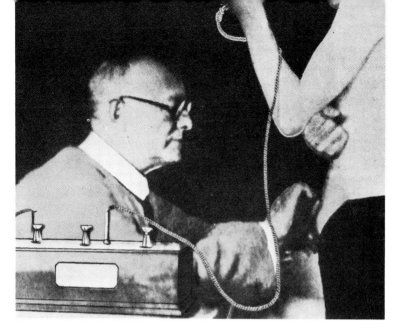

Dr Albert Abrams percussing a patient connected to one of his early diagnostic instruments.

Abrams next tested his discovery on a group of healthy subjects. He found that if a healthy person, facing west, held or was placed near a piece of diseased tissue the familiar dull note emanated from the abdomen on percussion. Take away the disease specimen and percussion produced the hollow resonance of health.

Abrams now wanted to find out if it was necessary for him to be in direct contact with the subject. Again using a group of healthy people he devised a 'blind' experiment. A wire, attached to the forehead of a subject, led through a screen to Abrams' assistant who systematically held the end over a number of disease specimens, among them, cancer, syphilis and tuberculosis. Abrams then attempted to 'identify' the disease at the other end of the wire by noting which area of the abdomen emitted a dull note. This experiment, however, resulted in a problem for Abrams: how to distinguish between one disease and another when the cancer and syphilis 'witnesses' behind the screen both produced a dull note in the same area of the abdomen. Had Abrams not had the drive – and the

139

money – to attempt to solve it, radionics would probably have been a stillborn idea.

Abrams thought that the phenomenon might depend on electro-magnetism. He began experimenting with a variable resistor, a simple device which can indicate the electrical conductance of the skin. By attaching the resistor to a healthy subject who was holding a jar containing diseased tissue, he could, by varying the setting of the instrument, distinguish between cancer and syphilis. His discovery was dubbed ERA or the Electronic Reactions of Abrams.

After several years research Abrams refined ERA to such an extent that he was able to dispense with the disease 'witness' and replace it with a blood or hair sample from a diseased patient. Abrams concluded that the blood and hair, and probably the saliva and finger nails, became impregnated with the energy pattern or vibrations of the disease, and could be 'read' by anyone 'tuning in' to its frequency. Abrams also proposed that if illness could be diagnosed by this method then it followed that it could also be eliminated if the vibrations of the patient could be normalised.

Convinced that he had made a momentous discovery of immense benefit to mankind, Abrams began manufacturing diagnostic equipment which he variously named Reflexophones, Sphygmobiometers or Sphygmophones. Later, Abrams developed a treatment instrument, the Oscilloclast. This was an impressive-looking piece of equipment, not unlike an early radio receiver, with knobs and dials and meters, but entirely lacking a connection to any electrical power supply. The 'works', such as they were, were contained in a black box which gave rise to the derisory nickname the device eventually acquired.

Abrams' 'black boxes' aroused widespread interest among the medical profession in America. Apart from manufacturing and selling the machines, Abrams also taught doctors how to use them. For a period he rode on a wave of success, but his critics not only doubted the efficacy of his device, but were also miffed at this unholy marriage between commerce and medicine.

An encouraging, but damagingly ambiguous, assessment of Abrams' work was made by a group of British doctors and

The Abrams 'Oscilloclast'.
One set of wires was attached to the forehead of a healthy subject
and a second set went to a container holding a blood sample from
an ailing patient. Abrams percussed the healthy person's abdomen.
Any irregularities were said to indicate the nature of the illness of
the sick patient who had supplied the blood sample.

physicists led by Sir Thomas Horder – later Lord Horder –
Physician to the King. Horder's committee approached Professor W. E. Boyd, a Glasgow homoeopath and ERA practitioner
who had developed his own radionic device, the Emanometer.
Several tests suggested that percussion, allied to the Emanometer, was potentially valuable as a diagnostic aid. But the committee concluded that the position of the practising 'electronist'
(Horder's name for the likes of Abrams and his followers) was
'scientifically unsound' and 'ethically unjustified'.

The possibility, always remote, that radionics might be taken
up by the orthodox medical profession in Britain was effectively
halted by the Horder Report. The death of Abrams in 1924 also
caused a hiatus in the development of radionics in its country of
origin. But in both countries there were individuals tending

141

radionics like a withering plant that seemed worth preserving. It is curious that both in the United States and in Britain radionics has been the cause of two minor legal 'causes célèbres'.

In America the guardian of radionics after Abrams' death was a chiropractor named Ruth Beymer Drown. Ruth Drown refined Abrams' machines and, although they remained essentially 'black boxes', she developed a method for using them for diagnosis *and* treatment. Ruth Drown has been a martyr to the cause of radionics since 1950 when her work led to a charge of fraud. Positive evidence about the healing achievements of Ruth Drown and her radionic instruments did not protect her from a guilty verdict. Her instruments were destroyed and she was briefly imprisoned. She died in 1966.

In Britain in 1960 George de la Warr, whose company manufactures radionic instruments, was alleged to have defrauded a woman who had bought one of his instruments but who proved incompetent to use it. De la Warr won the case, but it gained a notoriety for 'black boxes' in Britain which has not yet been lived down.

Radionics: analysis and treatment Radionics is most closely related to healing; indeed it would be difficult to maintain that radionics is not healing. It is, if you like, absent healing. However, a question often put to radionic practitioners is, 'If radionics is healing, what is the purpose of radionic instruments?' To a radionic practitioner, broadcast treatment is more accurate than healing by the laying on of hands. A radionic instrument enables the operator first to diagnose the complaint and its cause, and then to broadcast treatment. It is possible to dispense with instrumentation, but most radionic practitioners are not hand-healers; they find that their instruments enable them to treat more patients and a wider range of illnesses.

All that a practitioner requires to begin diagnosis or analysis of a patient's condition is a witness – usually a sample of blood, hair, or nails; some practitioners distrust blood as a witness because of the possibility that an overlooked blood transfusion will confuse them. Many radionic patients do not meet the practitioner, but a relationship by letter or telephone is estab-

Radiesthesia and Radionics

lished; this in itself some patients find beneficial. Most practitioners ask their patients to complete a form setting out the nature and duration of their complaint, the present symptoms and conditions and an account of any previous orthodox or other treatment they have received.

The practitioner starts his analysis of a new patient by placing his 'witness' on his instrument, his primary aim being to analyse the patient's overall state of health. The practitioner knows what the patient is suffering from, but what he must attempt to discover before treatment can begin is why the patient has the disease. One widely used instrument has three rows of eight dials and several other switches, a magnet, and a well in which the witness is placed. The practitioner holds his pendulum over the witness posing precise, silent questions and adjusts the dials in accordance with the answers he receives. To the radionic practitioner, his instrumental analysis is equivalent to the medical dowser or radiesthetist using pendulum and rule. The late Malcolm Rae, who modernised the approach of radionics in the sixties and designed several radionic instruments, suggested that the purpose of the initial analysis was to measure 'the amount of divergence between a thought representing perfection of a selected facet of the patient, and the thought pattern representing that facet's current condition in the patient'.

Other instruments rely on a 'stick pad' instead of a pendulum. The 'stick pad' is a rubber membrane on which the practitioner places the tips of his fingers. As he asks questions he lightly draws his fingers across the pad. He continues to do this until his fingers 'drag' on the membrane. This is the radionic equivalent of the positive reaction from the dowser's instrument. Imagine the practitioner is assessing a case of ulcerative colitis. With his knowledge of physiology, a qualified practitioner will know that it could be caused by a dysfunction in one of several organs, dietary abuse, or the illness could have a psychological basis. His questions typically would be: 'Is the spleen involved?', 'Is the patient suffering from an ulcer?', 'Has tension in the patient's life brought on the colitis?' The questions continue until the practitioner is satisfied that he has located the underlying causes of the patient's illness. During the questioning he might have experienced sticking or dragging

143

in response to, say, three questions out of twelve. Those practitioners who prefer to use a pendulum will ask similar questions, and will receive answers from the direction of its movement or the strength of its oscillation.

Having arrived at a radionic assessment of the patient's illness and its causes, the practitioner normally would consult his book of 'rates'. 'Rates' represent the figures to which the instrument should be 'tuned' to broadcast healing radiations which match the patient's complaint. They have been calculated by an experienced practitioner who, working with a pendulum and countless questions and answers, arrives at the optimum readings or settings on the instruments dials for all the most frequent complaints. Additionally, a practitioner would almost certainly place a homoeopathic remedy, if this is indicated, on the machine together with the patient's witness.

Radionic practitioners believe that they have improved the usual method of producing homoeopathic remedies (described on pp. 52–54) with a device called a Potency Simulator, another invention of the late Malcolm Rae. The claims made

The settings on the radionic instruments are changed two or three times every day to allow each instrument to be shared by more than one patient.

for this simple device are extraordinary. The Potency Simulator is said to be able to manufacture any potency of any homoeopathic remedy within minutes by using cards representing the geometric pattern of the remedy.

David V. Tansley, a leading practitioner and radionic theorist, believes that radionics works because it is treating not only the physical body, but what he calls the 'subtle anatomy' or the 'etheric body'. Believing this, he finds it essential to treat the *chakras* or force centres of the body. The Hindu belief is that the *chakras* are the centres of force where energy comes into the body. There are seven major and twenty-one minor chakras and, according to Tansley, they have three functions:

- To vitalise the physical body.
- To bring about the development of self-consciousness
- To transmit spiritual energy in order to bring the individual into a state of spiritual being.

They are, he says, 'in the nature of distributing agencies, providing dynamic force and qualitative energy to the body and produce definite effects upon the outward physical appearance.' David Tansley concedes that the chakra theory is 'too esoteric for most people to accept', but he claims that he has become more effective as a radionics practitioner since he consciously began applying his knowledge of the significance of the chakras. 'I recently had a case from Holland. I was sent only a photograph, nothing else. I sent back an analysis based on radionic examination of the chakras. The patient replied that the assessment was substantially correct.'

Does radionics work? If you are thinking that radionics is a bizarre kind of treatment which cannot possibly work, then you are not alone. Most people are sceptical or frankly dismissive about it. Even the Radionic Association which represents about eighty practitioners in Britain finds it difficult to discover how successful its members are in treating disease. The Association attempted a survey in 1976, which showed a 60 per cent success rate although only half the number of registered practitioners replied. During the production of the Anglia Television series, *The Medicine Men*, all listed members of the Radionic

145

Association were sent a questionnaire containing five questions designed to assess their success rate during a period of two years. Only half of the practitioners contacted replied and their replies confirm the earlier survey. The most common complaints were backache and spinal problems, psychological troubles – predominantly anxiety and depression – and allergies and skin complaints.

It would be easy to demolish radionics and confidently assert that much of what its practitioners believe and do is mumbo jumbo. That is the probable response of more people than would express total confidence in it. But how are we to regard those people who claim that they were helped towards recovery by radionic treatment, often after all other forms of medical evidence had failed? Case histories are not so reliable as evidence of effectiveness in radionics because many practitioners also simultaneously use other treatments, usually homoeopathy. It was noticeable that when practitioners claimed success – they are careful never to say that they have 'cured' anybody – the treatment lasted a comparatively long time, often more than a year. Does this mean that the patient was helped towards recovery simply through association with another caring human being? In other words, was the patient helped from within rather than from without? Would recovery have occurred without the help of pendulum analysis and broadcast treatment? Practitioners mostly would not deny that radionics can and often does work in this way, but they would claim that, like hand healers, they can be successful without the belief and co-operation of the patient.

Puzzled though we may be, irritated perhaps by the lack of hard scientific evidence proving cause and effect, suspicious of the need and efficacy or even necessity, of radionic hardware, it's possible tentatively to conclude that, like palmistry, astrology and ESP 'there may be something in it'.

Acupuncture

To administer medicines for diseases which have already developed is comparable to making weapons after the battle has begun.

The Yellow Emperor's Classic of Internal Medicine

The concept of whole health, a comparatively novel idea in Western countries, has for centuries provided the governing basis for Chinese medicine. The ancient Chinese knew about psychosomatic illness. They knew that a sick mind can cause the body to become sick; they knew also that a diseased body could not contain a totally healthy mind. The Chinese recognise, and not only in medicine, that all things are connected and interdependent. Balance is all.

Since the diplomatic breakthrough in the early seventies the Chinese, with their characteristic caution, have been moving towards a system of health care which marries the best in traditional medicine with western scientific medicine. It is inconceivable that they would discard traditional medicine in favour of imported medicine because that would deny balance. And the Chinese, it seems, are just as concerned as we are to avoid contaminating their bodies with chemical drugs.

The Chinese medical profession is at once irritated and amused that Western people (perhaps they lack balance) fail to understand that acupuncture represents only a part of Chinese medicine. No doubt Western doctors would feel misjudged if it was thought that their medicine relied only on injecting sick people with powerful drugs.

The other major element in practical Chinese medicine – herbalism – is similar to that widely practised in Europe until the arrival of chemical drugs. And the importance of diet and exercise, the other cornerstones of Chinese medicine, is, at least partially accepted in the West. Before prescribing herbal medicine or acupuncture a Chinese doctor would have to satisfy himself that the illness was not caused by, say, poor diet,

149

lack of exercise, or an imbalance in personal relationships.

Whether we are right or wrong to be primarily attracted to just one aspect of Chinese medicine, the truth is that we are. The West 'bought' acupuncture in the sixties because it was a clean and drugless therapy bolstered by an ancient and attractive theory which seemed strangely relevant to the second half of the twentieth century.

Acupuncture, Ancient and Modern

Acupuncture – derived from the Latin words *acus* (needle) and *punctura* (puncture) is a therapeutic system which relies on pucturing the skin at certain defined points in order to stimulate a 'vital' or healing energy to pass, via the nervous system, along invisible channels known as meridians to the diseased or painful part or organ.

Most modern acupuncturists employ techniques and observe certain theories about the function of the body that originated in China between two and three thousand years ago. We still do not know how the ancient Chinese discovered that pricking the skin with a needle in one area of the body had a therapeutic effect on another part. It's been suggested that acupuncture started after unexpected cures had been experienced by warriors injured in battle: a soldier injured in the leg might have found that his backache disappeared. Whatever its

The 'Nei Ching Su Wen' – *The Yellow Emperor's Classic of Internal Medicine.*

origin the theory and practice of acupuncture developed piecemeal for many centuries, but it was not until about 400 BC that it was formalised as a system of medicine in the 'Nei Ching Su Wen' or *The Yellow Emperor's Classic of Internal Medicine*. This book, the work of several authors and editors, established acupuncture within the context of traditional Chinese medicine. Much of the book is concerned with the philosophy of medicine and health and contains many ideas which find an echo in the twentieth century movement away from the powerful drugs and invasive techniques of Western medicine.

To the Chinese all things are either positive or negative. They are either *yang* (positive and male) or *yin* (negative and female). The ancient texts do not accord superiority to either *yin* or *yang*; after all, only equals can balance. Harmony of mind and body can only be achieved and maintained if *yin* and *yang*

The *t'ai chi t'u*. The Chinese symbol representing the balance of *yin* and *yang*.

are balanced. We can conceive of a 'balance' in a person, meaning someone who is sober, reliable and mature displaying no extremes in his temperament, character, or behaviour, but most of us would have difficulty in regarding the internal organs of the body in this way. We can, perhaps, accept that the seasons of the year and the elements have dominant characteristics which can loosely be labelled male and positive, or female and negative.

YANG (Male/Positive)	*YIN* (Female/Negative)
Sun	Moon
Sky	Earth
Fire	Water
Mountain	Valley
Summer	Winter

151

The internal organs of the body are also characterised as either *yin* or *yang*. The *yang* organs can be said to be mostly containers or tubes – the 'hollow' organs like the stomach, gall bladder, intestines and so on. The *yin* organs, perhaps the more vital group, comprise, for example, the heart, liver, and kidneys. If this strikes you as a somewhat crude division, it is. You don't have to be Chinese to know that people, places, and things are often neither wholly male or wholly female. So it is with the internal organs in Chinese medicine. Predominantly *yin* organs have some *yang* characteristics and vice versa.

The task of the ancient Chinese medicine man was to maintain a patient's *yin* and *yang* in a state of equilibrium. He could rely on a steady income so long as his patients remained healthy. If a patient became ill not only did his fees cease, but the 'doctor' would also have to provide out of his own pocket the cost of any medicines he prescribed in order to restore the patient's health. No more effective system of payment by incentives can ever have been devised.

Health depended not only on ensuring that the forces of *yin* and *yang* were balanced, but also that all parts of the body regularly received a vigorous and uninterrupted supply of *chi*. *Chi* can be regarded as 'vital energy' or 'life force', the equivalent of the Hindu *prana* or breath. *Chi* is distributed around the body along what can be imagined as a network of channels which acupuncturists call meridians. There are six *yang* meridians and six *yin* meridians:

YANG MERIDIANS	YIN MERIDIANS
Stomach	Spleen
Bladder	Kidney
Gall bladder	Liver
Large intestine	Lung
Small intestine	Heart
'Triple warmer'	Pericardium

'Triple warmer' has never been precisely identified or explained, but it's thought to refer to respiration, digestion, and reproduction. The 'pericardium' is concerned with the circulation of the blood.

Additionally and more obscurely, there are also two other

meridians known as the 'Governing Vessel' which follows approximately the route of the spine while the 'Conception Vessel' can be imagined as a vertical line down the middle of the front of the body. As acupuncture evolved other meridians were discovered, but modern practice is mostly concerned with the fourteen major meridians.

An essential part of the acupuncturist's equipment is a knowledge of the five elements: Fire, Earth, Metal, Water and Wood. The ancient Chinese texts claim that the circulation of *chi* along the meridians to the various organs of the body reflects the cyclic relationship of the five elements. That the elements are in constant interaction with each other can be seen in the two vital cycles: the Cycle of Generation (in which each element creates a new element) and the Cycle of Destruction (in which each element destroys the succeeding element).

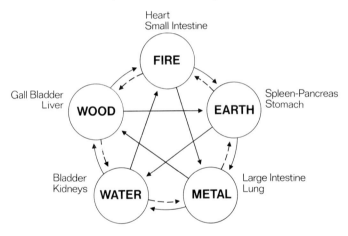

The Chinese see the constant interaction of the five elements (fire, earth, metal, water and wood) as a vital part of the workings of the body.

CYCLE OF GENERATION
FIRE makes EARTH (ash)
EARTH yields METAL
METAL produces WATER (molten metal?)
WATER produces WOOD (growth)
WOOD makes FIRE

153

CYCLE OF DESTRUCTION
FIRE destroys METAL (melting)
METAL destroys WOOD (cutting)
WOOD absorbs EARTH (growth)
EARTH absorbs WATER (drainage)
WATER destroys FIRE (extinguishes)

The cyclic association of the five elements is not too difficult for Western minds to accept. We may, however, find it more difficult to follow the ancient Chinese belief that each of the five elements is identified with the organs of the body. Thus:

FIRE   – Heart, small intestine, 'triple heater' and pericardium
EARTH   – Stomach, spleen
METAL   – Large intestine, lungs
WATER   – Bladder, kidneys
WOOD   – Liver, gall bladder

The law of the five elements is not merely an historical curiosity, but is part of acupuncture practice. There are points on each meridian representing the five elements. By stimulating, say, a 'Metal' point the large intestine or the lungs (the 'Metal' organs) can be either stimulated or sedated. Some practitioners admit that when treatment fails it is sometimes because the significance of the five elements has been ignored.

Pulse diagnosis As with other systems of whole medicine, the acupuncturist is interested to find out what made you ill or, perhaps, why you allowed yourself to become ill. The homoeopath with his questions about likes and dislikes is mirrored by the acupuncturist who relies not on the subjective answers to questions, but on the evidence provided by the pulse.

The acupuncturist uses his hands to do the work of the complicated and highly expensive scientific machinery found in most large hospitals. By taking the pulse at the radial artery in both wrists the acupuncturist can monitor the activity of the twelve 'meridian organs' in the body.

There are six pulse points on each wrist and an acupuncturist making a diagnosis will feel the 'superficial' pulse with light pressure followed by stronger pressure to assess the pulse at a deeper level. He might note your heart rate while feeling your pulse, but he is more interested in sensing any disturbances or irregularities in the rhythm at both levels.

Acupuncture is very definitely not a 'do it yourself' technique, but it is possible by placing a finger at three adjacent positions on the radial artery at least to accept that the 'tone' of the pulse, but not its rate, differs at the three surface points. Even experienced acupuncturists find it difficult to monitor irregularities at the deeper level, but they claim that pulse diagnosis is often more accurate than the question and answer technique of the orthodox doctor, and can identify not only current illness, but also past and future ill-health.

Pulse diagnosis usually confirms the patient's own account of his state of health. If he has a known ailment it can be detected in the pulse. If he complains of a non-specific pain in the chest or a headache, pulse diagnosis will provide further evidence about the cause of the pain. Acupuncturists describe irregularities in a pulse in everyday language; they use words like 'hollow', 'wiry', 'coarse' and so on. Once the acupuncturist is satisfied that he has identified the seat of the complaint he can begin treatment.

Acupuncturists, like other doctors, augment physical and visual examination with 'taking the case'. An old Chinese medical text sets out ten questions – known as the Ten Askings – to be used in the clinical assessment of a new patient. They would not be out of place in a modern textbook for doctors.

> 'One ask chill and fever, two perspiration, three ask head and trunk, four stool and urine, five food intake and six chest. Deafness and thirst are seven and eight, nine past history and ten causes. Besides this, you should ask about the drugs taken and for women you should ask the menstrual and obstetric history. Finally for infants ask about normal childhood diseases.'

Because of the difficulty of mastering it, the ancient system of pulse diagnosis has been abandoned by many practitioners in favour of a simpler and more rational method not dissimilar

155

from the orthodox pulse-rate assessment. The modern method is called 'pulse generalisation' and, by comparison with the ancient method, is no more than a superficial assessment of the tone of the pulse. But acupuncturists who use 'pulse generalisation', allied to observing the condition and appearance of the tongue and normal case-taking, claim that their diagnostic results are quicker but no less accurate than the ancient method.

Treatment Having diagnosed the complaint the acupuncturist is faced with choosing from over three hundred points on the meridians where to place the needles. The skill of the acupuncturist lies in selecting those points which he knows from his training and experience will stimulate the healing processes. What the acupuncturist seeks to do is to trip the switch that leads to recovery by applying the minimum amount of stimulation.

How, then, does the acupuncturist navigate his way along these invisible pathways, the meridians, so that he punctures the skin precisely at the point laid down in the textbooks for a particular complaint? The question of accuracy in needling is one that continues to exercise practitioners, but the short answer is that the acupuncturist plots his selection of points largely on the basis of empirical experience. He 'knows' for example, that needling the Liver meridian behind the knee on the right leg, either alone or together with other points at the base of the neck on the gall bladder meridian, will often alleviate a migraine headache.

Acupuncture points often correspond with what orthodox medicine knows as 'trigger' points. They have been described as nodules, similar to those found in fibrositis, near to the surface of the skin. They are often painful to touch and an acupuncturist should always make an overall physical examination in order to find the sensitive points on the skin. This is a form of reverse diagnosis because having found the sensitive points he can often identify the complaint. These sensitive points – sometimes they might show up as larger areas of hard tissue just below the surface of the skin – are often sought by orthodox physicians who recognise them as symptomatic of certain diseases. If a patient complains of what seems to be a

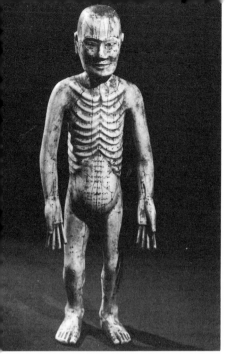
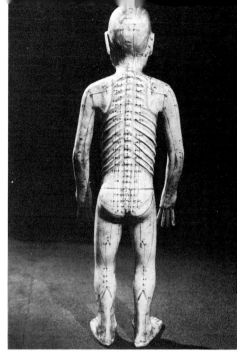

An early nineteenth-century papier mâché figure used for teaching
acupuncture points.

There are about 1,000 acupuncture points, of which about one-third
are commonly used. *Chi*, the life force, is said to flow along the
fourteen major meridians.

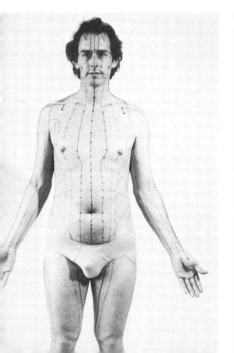
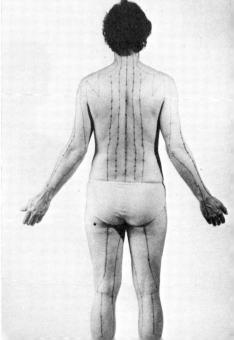

gall bladder disturbance he will nearly always have points of tenderness in the area of the right shoulder. These are acupuncture points, but are not of course recognised as such by orthodox physicians. Some acupuncturists believe that orthodox hypodermic injection and sometimes surgery, is a form of unconscious acupuncture. One of Britain's leading acupuncturists relates that a patient of his, a blood donor who suffered from persistent headache, experienced relief for about two hours after giving blood. The acupuncturist found that her blood was being drawn off from a point near the elbow which corresponded with the acupuncture point for treating her complaint.

Does acupuncture hurt? Acupuncture is often thought to be akin to injection by hypodermic syringe. But the hypodermic syringe is a crude instrument compared with the acupuncturist's needles. The syringe can have a relatively large diameter particularly if a large volume is to be injected. The hypodermic syringe is, of course, hollow, but the acupuncturist's needle is

Modern acupuncture needles are about ⅓ mm in diameter. Needles are generally inserted only 5–30 mm into the skin.

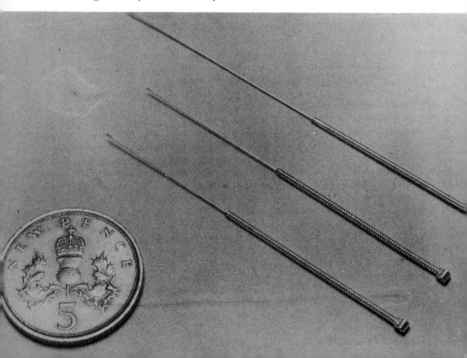

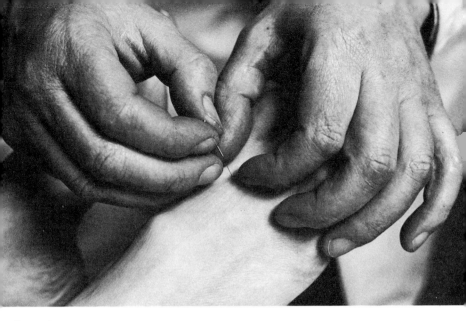

Insertion of an acupuncture needle is rarely painful.

like a fine stiletto, so fine that it could fit inside the shaft of a typical hypodermic syringe. Early acupuncture needles were made of stone, bamboo, gold, silver, or bronze, but modern acupuncturists mostly use sterilisable stainless steel needles with a diameter of 0.35mm.

In the hands of an experienced practitioner the needle simply divides the tissue of the skin to a depth of about 5–30mm usually without either drawing blood or causing pain. It is a common experience for an acupuncturist to be asked by the patient when the needles are going in only to be told that needling has already begun. Intending patients might be comforted by the knowledge that an accidental prick from a pin is likely to be more painful than acupuncture.

After the needles have been inserted the acupuncturist normally inquires if the patient is feeling any sensation either at the acupuncture points or elsewhere in the body. If acupuncture is going to work the patient normally reports that the area around the needles has gone 'numb' or that a similar sensation is being felt some distance away from the acupuncture point. If this remote sensation is anywhere on a meridian 'connected' to the chosen acupuncture point the practitioner can be reasonably confident that the treatment is going to take effect.

159

Another typical reaction, one that often accompanies successful homoeopathic treatment, is that needling causes the symptoms temporarily to worsen before they get better.

Puncturing the skin alone sometimes produces a strong reaction, but most acupuncturists attempt to stimulate a response by rotating the needle either continuously or at intervals during the needling which usually last for 10–20 minutes. After a needling sensation has been obtained some practitioners connect the needles to an electrical stimulator.

Acupuncture sometimes affords almost instantaneous relief from pain, but this should not be thought to be the norm. It is more common for a gradual alleviation of symptoms to occur over a period of two to three months; weekly treatments are recommended, but longer intervals between needling will not render acupuncture ineffective. Most acupuncturists agree that if no improvement has been effected in a patient's condition after three or four treatments then it is unlikely that acupuncture will work at all. After a successful course of 8–10 treatments a patient should be able to enjoy up to about six months free of pain or symptoms, but a course of 'booster' treatments is then usually required.

Moxibustion

As an alternative, or in addition to needling, some acupuncturists employ a technique of warming the acupuncture points known as moxibustion. It is often used by 'barefoot doctors' – China's paramedical corps – to restore balance to a body adversely affected by cold. Moxa – made from the herb *Artemisia vulgaris* or Mugwort – is first dried and then powdered before it is ready for use.

The most common moxibustion treatment consists of igniting a small cone of moxa and allowing it to smoulder on or close to the chosen acupuncture point. It is removed when the patient feels the heat and, possibly, some pain. A refinement of the cone technique is to place a piece of garlic, ginger, or salt over the point and then light the moxa; this has the effect of prolonging the transfer of heat to the patient.

Moxa is also made into small sticks which are lit and placed on or close to the skin; the patient is expected to be able to

160

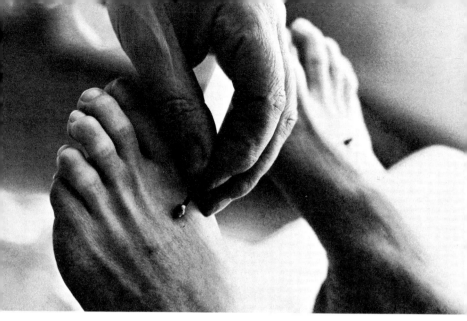

A small cone of the herb, moxa, smoulders to warm an acupuncture point.

tolerate the heat although the skin should not be blistered. Moxa is also sometimes used to heat acupuncture needles during treatment.

Acupuncture Anaesthesia

In the West, public consciousness of acupuncture was established in the early seventies by astonishing pictures purporting to show major surgery being performed on smiling Chinese patients who, though fully conscious, had been anaesthetised by acupuncture. Medical delegations from Britain and the United States returned full of enthusiasm although there were sceptics among them. They suspected that they might have been part of a public relations exercise designed to show to the world the medical delights available to Chinese citizens under Chairman Mao's venerable leadership.

Dr George Lewith, Lecturer in Primary Medical Care at the University of Southampton and a practising acupuncturist, spent nearly a year in China in 1979 and witnessed over fifty operations under acupuncture anaesthesia. He became accustomed to seeing Chinese patients displaying indifference as the surgeon removed an appendix or explored his liver or stomach.

161

He was satisfied that effective analgesia was induced in many patients although there were some failures. He concluded that the failure rate, low though it was, and the considerable time required to induce analgesia or anaesthesia makes the method unacceptable to Western patients.

One British consultant anaesthetist is, however, using a combination of acupuncture and drugs on patients for whom a general anaesthetic might be dangerous.

Another comparatively new technique now widely used by the Chinese is ear acupuncture. *The Barefoot Doctor's Manual*, the handbook of China's paramedics, suggests that there are 110 points on the ear which can be used not only for analgesia but also in the treatment of about seventy ailments, among them

Needling of the ear acupuncture points has been found to affect the organs corresponding to the anatomy of a human foetus superimposed on the ear.

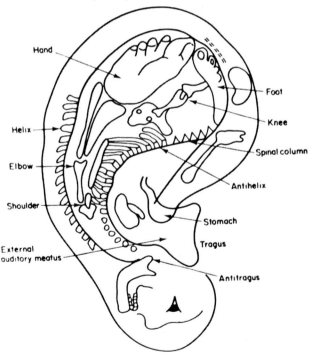

tonsillitis, dysmenorrhea and hiccups. The theory is that the appearance of the external ear is similar to an inverted foetus; a pathological condition in any part of the body will be represented by an area of tenderness or increased electrical conductance in the external ear.

This may sound fanciful, but a research project at the University College of Los Angeles School of Medicine tends to support the hypothesis. Forty patients were medically examined to find out where they suffered any musculo-skeletal pain. Each patient, draped in a sheet to conceal any obvious physical problems, was given an 'ear diagnosis' by another physician who had no prior knowledge of their condition. The purpose of the ear diagnosis was to locate any area of tenderness or increased electrical conductance. It was found that ear diagnosis confirmed the orthodox diagnosis in thirty of the forty patients, a result that could not be dismissed as a chance occurrence.

How Does Acupuncture Work?

The cause of acupuncture would be considerably advanced if it could be explained in terms of modern scientific theory. But there has been comparatively little research into acupuncture in the West probably because the prejudiced view of most scientists – that it is a curious medical also-ran – is deeply entrenched in all but a handful of medical researchers in America, Britain and Japan. In China, research has not yet attained the sophistication of Western science, possibly because the pragmatic Chinese, with 900-million people to care for, are obliged to direct their funds and their energies towards practical rather than theoretical medicine.

Most recent research in Britain and the United States has been directed towards proving the supposition that acupuncture is directly related to the nervous body's central and autonomic system. This approach got under way in the mid-sixties, almost as a by-product of mainstream orthodox neurological research. It was proposed that there was an imaginary barrier between the site of a pain and the brain. Now this checkpoint usually allowed pain signals to pass uninterrupted via the

163

nervous system up the spinal cord to the brain. It was discovered that acupuncture had the effect of stopping pain messages getting through; it was also suggested that needling interrupted the brain's 'memory' of pain. This research, known as the 'gate theory', won the Nobel Prize for Professor Ronald Melzack of McGill University and Professor Patrick Wall of London University. They proposed that acupuncture stimulated the larger nerves in the body to close the 'gate', effectively anaesthetising that part of the body which was transmitting 'I am in pain' messages. To practising acupuncturists the 'gate theory' was only partially satisfactory. It explained what happened to the body during acupuncture, but not why its pain-relieving effects continued long after needling.

Acupuncture research took a major step forward in the mid-seventies with the discovery that the body contains, or is able to manufacture, pain-killing substances known as endorphins. Endorphins are produced by many parts of the endocrine system, as well as the pituitary gland, more or less when we need them, to help us cope with stress, pain, or injury. They are always present, but production varies according to the body's changing requirements. Of course, endorphins are not the exclusive preserve of acupuncture, but their function tended to support those who had long made the unsubstantiated claim that acupuncture stimulated some naturally occurring function of the body's nervous system.

The main thrust of endorphin research is directed towards finding ways of stimulating and controlling their function in the body. Think of the boon that this would be to the countless people who suffer constant or intermittent acute pain from, say, migraine, if they could be provided with the means of calling up their own built-in pain control service. Experiments in several countries have shown that endorphin production goes up when the body is given a weak electrical stimulus which approximates to the stimulation given by an acupuncture needle.

At St Bartholomew's Hospital Medical School, London, a research team working with a group in Hong Kong compared the endorphin content in the spinal fluid of a group of ten patients suffering recurrent pain with another ten subjects who were pain-free. Spinal fluid samples taken from both groups prior to electro-acupuncture showed similar levels of endor-

Acupuncture, augmented by a minimum amount of anaesthetic drugs, was used during a hip replacement operation on this eighty-year-old woman in an NHS hospital. She was unable to have a general anaesthetic because of a severe chest condition.

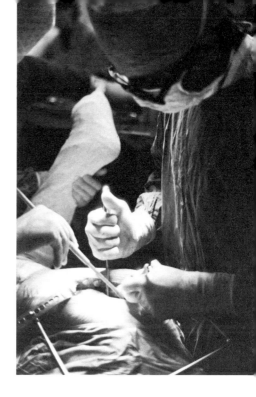

In the pre-operative room an electrical pulse stimulator enhances the anaesthetic effects of the needles in her leg.

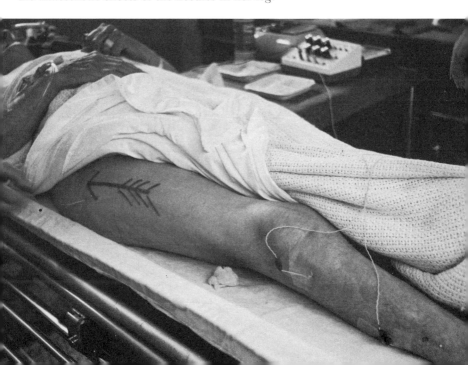

phins. Electro-acupuncture for a period of 20–30 minutes had no effect on the 'pain-free' group, but produced a significant rise in the endorphin levels of the 'pain' group. Pain relief in all ten subjects lasted from 30 minutes to two days. The result of this experiment and other research suggests that the analgesic agent is being produced within the body. The researchers find it significant that nalaxone – a drug widely used as an antidote to hard drugs – also reverses some of the pain-killing effects of acupuncture. So, if nalaxone inhibits the analgesic effects of both hard drugs and the endorphins produced by acupuncture, it seems likely that the analgesia was caused by the endorphins.

Endorphins produce effects similar to those obtained from morphine or heroin; heroin addicts are known to have below-average levels of endorphin-like compounds in their spinal fluid. We know now that acupuncture raises the levels of these substances and this probably explains why acupuncture has been found to be an effective treatment for the withdrawal syndrome in drug addicts in Hong Kong. In Britain, Dr Margaret Patterson, who learned to treat drug addiction with acupuncture in Hong Kong, has developed a simple electronic device which enables a low-frequency electrical current to pass through electrodes attached to both sides of the head close to the ears. Dr Patterson has had considerable success, but why the treatment should work is far from clear, although it's almost certainly related to endorphin activity.

Other researchers tested the not unreasonable premise that endorphins provided a scientific explanation of hypnosis, but their findings indicated that hypnosis and endorphins were unrelated; neither was acupuncture analgesia a form of hypnosis. An hypnotic trance can be induced within 30–60 seconds to such a depth that a subject can accept a surgical needle inserted in the skin on the back of the hand, but acupuncture analgesia only takes effect after about twenty minutes needling when endorphin levels have reached an effective level and are then able to inhibit pain. Since every practitioner can cite cases where needling produced an almost instantaneous relief of a condition, this suggests that endorphins do not provide a complete explanation of acupuncture.

There is general agreement amongst acupuncturists that neither the 'gate theory' nor endorphins provides the final answer to how and why the needles work. While it's accepted that acupuncture can alleviate backache or rheumatism by eliminating the sensation of pain, we still do not know how it can relieve asthma or sinusitis.

What Complaints Respond to Acupuncture?

There have been relatively few clinical trials of acupuncture and those that have been completed do not provide totally reliable evidence on which to base large claims for its efficacy. Acupuncturists do not shout loudly about their frequent successes, but most can tell of remarkable recoveries by patients suffering from illnesses which conventional medicine had failed to cure. In general, acupuncture offers a reliable alternative method of treatment for most of the ailments regularly presented to an orthodox general practitioner.

The World Health Organisation (WHO) is championing the wider use of acupuncture as it becomes increasingly clear that Western scientific medicine is inapplicable to much of the Third World on the grounds of cost and the widespread, instinctive resistance to pill-based medicine. A recent WHO seminar in Peking claimed that while acupuncture was not to be regarded as a panacea for all ills it had application to diseases in most parts of the body.

The following classification of diseases which are known to respond in some degree to acupuncture is based on the conclusions of the WHO seminar and the clinical experience of several British acupuncturists:

Respiratory system Acute sinusitis, acute rhinitis, common cold, acute tonsilitis, acute bronchitis, bronchial asthma. The treatment of asthma in children is particularly successful.

A young boy was treated for asthma at the College of Traditional Acupuncture in Leamington Spa. He had almost continuous lethargy which led to frequent absence from school and his removal to a special school was being considered. After a standard course of treatment with occasional boosters the boy's asthma abated and he became normal in energy and achievement. Orthodoxy might claim that this was due to

167

'spontaneous remission', but the boy's parents ascribe it wholly to acupuncture.

Gastro-intestinal disorders Gastric and duodenal ulcers (by reducing the level of acidity in the stomach); spasms of the oesophagus; hiccups; acute and chronic gastritis; gastric hyperacidity; acute and chronic colitis; acute dysentery; constipation; diarrhoea; irritable bowel; gall stones.

Disorders of the nervous system Headaches; migraine; neuralgia; facial palsy (if treated early enough); stroke; Ménière's disease; nocturnal enuresis; facial pain; facial paralysis (Bell's Palsy); shingles.

Ménière's disease was diagnosed in a young married woman who complained of giddiness, loss of balance, tinnitus (noises in the ear), lethargy and depression. Acupuncture did not effect a complete cure, but relieved the giddiness and the tinnitus and led to a general improvement in her overall condition.

Another patient, a man suffering from almost daily migraine headaches of varying intensity, is in no doubt that acupuncture has enabled him to live free of pain and without the debilitating side-effects produced by his former high intake of pain-killing drugs.

Bone, joint, and muscle disorders Frozen shoulder; tennis elbow; sciatica; low back pain; osteo-arthritis; rheumatoid arthritis.

Following a sports injury, a man in his mid-thirties developed severe neck pain. His condition was not improved by two operations and the pain could only be kept under control by large amounts of pain-killers, including heroin. He was given a course of ten treatments of ear and body acupuncture. Within two months his pain disappeared and he no longer required pain-killers. He now leads a normal, pain-free life; any recurrence is controlled by occasional booster treatments.

The importance of booster treatments is exemplified by another case from the files of the same practitioner. A lady of almost seventy with arthritis in both knees was able to retain mobility only by pain-killing and anti-rheumatic drugs, but eventually this treatment was insufficient to control the pain.

Acupuncture did not rid the patient of her pain, but it was brought under control, and treatments every three or four months enable her to lead an almost pain-free life.

Consulting an Acupuncturist

As with other alternative therapies which are available through doctors and lay practitioners, acupuncture has its divisions and jealousies. Some doctors are outraged that anyone without a medical training should dare to attempt to heal the sick. Lay practitioners, for their part, claim with some justification that their training is often superior. Most lay acupuncturists have studied the subject for at least three years, but many doctor-acupuncturists are either self-taught or they have attended only brief courses. You may feel safer placing yourself in the hands of a doctor who has the fail-safe option of turning to orthodox medicine, but if you want acupuncture it makes sense to consult a practitioner who has the widest knowledge and experience of acupuncture irrespective of other qualifications.

Anyone who studies acupuncture for several years will be knowledgeable not only about pulses and meridians, but will also have acquired a considerable familiarity with anatomy and physiology, the basis of an orthodox medical training. It is for this reason and also because acupuncture does not easily lend itself to exclusivity that some doctor-acupuncturists welcome the contribution made by lay practitioners, not only in providing a service in parts of the country where it would otherwise be unavailable, but also by their enthusiasm in keeping acupuncture buoyant. Dr Lewith believes that lay practitioners are often as good as, if not better than, some medically qualified acupuncturists.

A Liverpool acupuncturist, Dr Julian Kenyon, agrees, but warns that some lay practitioners lack clinical judgement and may continue treatment when the proper course would be to refer the patient for conventional treatment. Doctors, says Dr Kenyon, should not make this kind of error. However, he admits that despite his experience of acupuncture he is willing to learn from lay practitioners. 'The Chinese,' he says, 'teach you to be much less arrogant, to accept sound medical knowledge from whatever source it might come.'

If you are comforted by the knowledge that you have entrusted your body for treatment to a medically qualified acupuncturist you narrow your choice to about 150 practitioners. Most of them belong to the British Medical Acupuncture Society whose members can only be approached by referral from another doctor. If your doctor is unwilling to have truck with acupuncture the only recourse for the determined patient is to change doctors. As transferring from one NHS doctor to another is not the simple matter it ought to be, you should consider consulting a lay acupuncturist privately.

Lay acupuncturists in Britain mostly qualify at one of three colleges: the British Acupuncture Association in London, the College of Traditional Chinese Acupuncture in Leamington Spa, and the International College of Oriental Medicine based at East Grinstead in Sussex. Further information about these organisations is in the reference section. It should not be thought that these colleges train only lay acupuncturists; all three colleges number doctors amongst their students.

It is more difficult to be accurate about the number of lay acupuncturists at work in Britain because not all of them are necessarily products of the three 'lay' colleges. Some highly effective acupuncturists cannot point to diplomas proudly displayed on the walls of their consulting rooms, but their prowess is witnessed by their packed appointment books, and no doubt their healthy bank accounts. Their reputations are spread by word of mouth. In the world of alternative medicine, this can often be a far more accurate guide to reliability than a piece of fading parchment.

Naturopathy

Your food should be your medicine
and your medicine food.

Hippocrates

We are all naturopaths. We all instinctively want to encourage
nature to cure our everyday injuries and illnesses. Sleep is
nature cure. Bathing is nature cure. Drinking water – even
recycled water – is nature cure. Taking prunes, rhubarb, bran
or bran products is nature cure. Coating a burn with butter is
nature cure. There are many other examples which even the
most confirmed of pill addicts would readily acknowledge.

Most of us, however, when suffering from a more serious
complaint would not think nature equal to the task of over-
coming it. We go to the doctor for a 'magic bullet' to eliminate
the illness. Naturopaths, on the other hand, believe that the
body must be given a chance. They believe in encouraging the
body to fight its own battles. They realise that the body needs
help, but not from alien chemicals. Their aim is to bring the
body to an optimum condition to enable it to cure itself.

If you consult a naturopath you will be expected to collabo-
rate in the cure of your complaint. Much of the responsibility
for recovery rests on the patient because naturopathic treatment is largely a matter of re-education. The patient is admit-
ting failure: he has so dealt with his life and his body that he has
made himself ill. This may seem harsh and uncompromising,
but naturopaths point out that treatment, at its simplest, relies
on nothing that is not available to the patient.

The naturopath assumes that the patient has, to a greater or
lesser degree, ignored the adage that 'you are what you eat' and
usually demands a revolution in living and dietary habits. It's a
measure of how far we have departed from 'natural living' that
a regime which requires us to stop smoking, reduce or give up
drinking, replace white bread with wholewheat bread, avoid or

A sixteenth-century bath house for women.

severely restrict salt, fats, and sugar would be seen by most of us as difficult if not impossible to implement. Additionally, the naturopath would require a patient to take regular exercise and to reduce stress at work and at home. If, says the naturopath, you can agree to follow this regime then you will feel better and, depending on its severity, you may recover wholly or partially from your complaint. It is one of the attractions of 'nature cure' that treatment, and therefore eventual recovery, is the responsibility of the patient, unlike orthodox medicine which often requires of the patient passive, unquestioning co-operation. In naturopathy, the practitioner guides; the patient controls.

Naturopaths believe that we would all be fitter, happier, and more efficient at working and at playing if we lived our lives in accordance with natural principles. Our avoidance or ignorance of these principles, they claim, is responsible for much of the illness to which man, particularly Western man, is prone. They claim that we abuse and neglect our bodies to such an extent that we make ourselves ill. If we don't get cancer from excessive smoking, we get heart trouble from laziness and too much fat or sugar or both. If we don't succumb to self-induced

174

illness from poor quality or 'junk food' we create a fertile breeding ground for disease. Naturopaths find very little to commend in the way most of us conduct our dietary lives.

Naturopaths are often accused of being killjoys and food faddists. This reputation might have been justified in the nineteenth century or the early decades of this century when practitoners who insisted on harsh regimes found many adherents, but it is untrue today. Certainly naturopaths eliminate from the diets of their patients much that is enjoyable, but today they do not apply the doctrine of the hair-shirt, but that of the whole man. This approach, shared in one form or another by all modern 'medicine men', seeks to return a person to a standard of health from which, as a result of working against rather than with nature, he has departed.

It is the view of naturopaths that they are doing in their small way what doctors should be doing as a matter of course. If doctors examined the diets of their patients and insisted, as naturopaths do, on a regular intake of whole, unadulterated food then much trivial illness would not occur.

The initiative must come from the doctors because they are still regarded as the most authoritative source of knowledge and advice on health. We have been conditioned to accept unquestioningly the medical advice we receive from them. If our doctor does not refer to diet we assume that it is neither relevant nor important. Any attempt to discuss diet is to risk being branded a 'difficult patient'. The average general practitioner does not subscribe to the view that 'you are what you eat' because his training has left him without the intellectual support for such an extreme or 'quacky' approach to health because most medical schools do not include nutrition in the curriculum.

You can count yourself very fortunate if your GP is interested in what you eat. The chances are that he gets by on much the same diet as his patients so food is not as significant to him as it is to the naturopath. It is a fundamental tenet of natural therapy that the body cannot begin to heal itself until it is fed regularly on whole food, produced on healthy soil which has not been treated with chemical fertilisers.

Get Moving!

Naturopaths and doctors interested in preventive medicine say exercise is essential for good health. Walking or cycling to work or regular gardening or swimming are all excellent ways to stay active. However, some people prefer to follow a set schedule of exercises. The programme on these pages has been devised by the Health Education Council:

Some tips:

* ★ Exercise regularly – a little every day, if possible.
* ★ Start with about ten repetitions for each of the exercises.
* ★ If you have any doubt about whether you should exercise, talk to your doctor first.

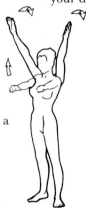

a

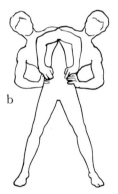

b

c

a. *Arm swinging*
Feet wide astride with arms loosely by your side. Raise both arms forward, upwards, backwards and sideways in a circular motion, brushing your ears with your arms as you go past.

b. *Side bends*
Feet wide apart with hands on hips. Bend first to your left, then to your right, keeping your head facing forwards all the time.

c. *Trunk, knee and hip bends*
Stand 18 in. behind the back of a chair with your hands resting lightly on the chair. Raise your left knee and bring your forehead down to meet it. Do the same with the right knee. This should be a long, strong, slow movement

176

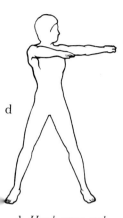

d. *Head, arms and trunk rotating*
Feet wide astride, hands and arms reaching directly forwards at shoulder level. Turn your head, arms and shoulder around to the left as far as you can go, bending the right arm across the chest, then repeat the movement to the right.

e. *Alternate ankle reach*
Feet wide apart with both palms on the front of the upper left thigh. Relax the trunk forward as you slide both hands down the front of your left leg. Return to upright position and repeat on the right. (If you suffer backache you must not pass the knees with your hands.)

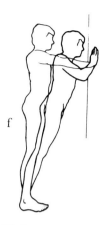

f. *Wall press-ups*
Stand with your hands on wall 12 in. apart at shoulder height with your arms straight. Stand on your toes, then bend your arms until your chest and chin touch the wall. Return to starting position by straightening your arms.

g. *Abdominal exercise*
Sit on the front part of the chair, legs straight, heels on the floor. Lean back and grip the sides of the seat for support. Bend your knees and bring your thighs up to squeeze gently against your body. Drop your legs back to the floor.

177

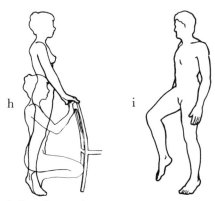

h. *Leg exercise*
Stand 18 in. behind chair with your hands on its back. Lower your body into a squat. Straighten both legs and come up on your toes.

i. *Running on the spot*
Do not raise your knees high initially, but aim to get them higher later. Start doing about 30 seconds and gradually increase.

Food – the Front Line of Naturopathy

Naturopaths are frequently accused of scaremongering with their assertion that nearly all commonly consumed foods are bad for you. Show us the benefit of so-called whole food, say the sceptics. Surely we are healthier than our parents and our grandparents? And so on. All this is conceded by the naturopaths, but they claim that a diet based on whole and raw food could arrest the incidence of preventable disease which has been inexorably rising almost from the beginning of the twentieth century.

Even allowing for the increase in population, the following statistics should be enough to convince the most diehard sceptic that food cannot escape suspicion as a prime cause:

- ★ Coronary thrombosis has doubled since 1945.
- ★ One in three 'healthy' people is suffering from a diagnosable complaint.
- ★ Nearly half of all adults have had all their teeth removed.
- ★ Every year four million teeth are extracted from British children.
- ★ One in four men and one in five women will develop cancer.
- ★ One in five men will suffer coronary heart disease.

> **INGREDIENTS** Sugar, Vegetable Fats with Antioxidant, Dextrose, Edible Starch, Emulsifiers, Salt, Colour, Sorbic Acid, Flavour, Stabiliser.

Lists of ingredients from a commonly available brand of packet cake mix. Naturopaths argue that fast foods are over-refined and tainted with chemical preservatives, colours, taste enhancers, flavourings and sweeteners which our bodies do not need.

> ★ At least half the population has some kind of digestive disorder.

Now if these statistics referred to animals – 'nearly half of all dogs have had their teeth removed' or 'one in five cats will develop cancer' – we should immediately suspect that they were poorly fed. When animals become sick the cause is invariably ascribed to food, but illness in their owners is almost never put down to eating habits.

A naturopath will normally insist that a patient makes a serious attempt to reform his diet so that a preponderance of whole food is eaten every day and at every meal. Most naturopaths recognise, however, that while patients find it impossible to make immediate and extreme changes in their diets, they will attempt to follow a programme of gradual improvement. To encourage new patients and to illustrate how easy reform of diet can be many naturopaths provide a meal by meal breakdown of permitted or recommended foods. There are variants on the basic maintenance diet to suit individual complaints, but most whole food diets will read something like this:

Breakfast
    Oatmeal porridge (about 25 grams (1 oz) dry oats per person) or muesli
    Egg or cheese
    Yoghourt
    Fresh fruit

Whole wheat bread or toast with thinly spread butter.
Marmalade (coarse-cut) or honey in moderation.
Weak tea or coffee, or coffee substitute, or fruit juice or
herb tea.

Most commercial products described as 'muesli' or 'Swiss
breakfast' bear almost no relation to the muesli devised by Dr
M. O. Bircher-Benner and still prescribed for most patients at
the Bircher-Benner Clinic in Zurich. It is a whole meal, and
should not be regarded as a predominantly cereal dish or as a
pudding. This is how to make a Bircher-Benner muesli:

One level tbs oats,
3 tbs water,
1 tbs lemon juice,
1 tbs (per person) sweetened con-
densed milk,
about 175 grams (7 ozs) apples,
1 tbs grated hazelnuts or almonds

Soak oats in water overnight, or for about 8–10 hours. Mix
lemon juice and condensed milk to a smooth cream. Mix cream
thoroughly with the soaked oats. Grate washed apples and stir
into mixture to prevent discolouration. Top with grated nuts
and serve immediately.

Midday meal

Vegetable salad. This is intended to be a substantial meal,
not just a few lettuce leaves and half a tomato. Choose a
combination of any of the following raw ingredients: cabbage, cauliflower, spinach, carrots, beetroot, parsnip,
turnip, Brussels sprouts, celery, leeks, mushrooms,
watercress, onions, peppers, sprouted beans.
Fruits – apples, bananas, oranges, grapes – can be added;
also cottage cheese or grated hard cheese, soaked raisins,
hard-boiled eggs, and nuts.
Whole wheat bread
Baked potato
Fresh fruit or yoghourt

Evening meal
   Soup – made from fresh ingredients
   Main dish – 100–150 grams (4–6 ozs) meat or fish, or a
   vegetarian dish made from pulses (beans), eggs, cheese,
   nuts, or vegetables.
   Vegetables – lightly cooked or steamed to preserve nutri-
   tive value.
   Raw vegetable salad.
   Fresh fruit or yoghourt.
   (The two main meals of the day are interchangeable)

   This regime, or something like it, will be recommended by
any naturopath to a patient who has been used to consuming a
conventional diet with probably excessive amounts of fats and
sugar. Most naturopaths insist that their patients avoid, or
severely restrict, their intake of all of the following foods:

   —Sugar – white and brown, and sugar cooked in cakes and
pastries. And you can't avoid the ban on sugar by taking the
equivalent amount of honey. At the very least, cut down your
sugar or honey intake to a minimum.
   —White flour and all white flour products. White bread,
biscuits, most commercial ice-cream, sweets and chocolates,
and packet desserts.
   —Excessive amounts of fats, oils, including butter.
   —Use fats and oils in cooking sparingly and spread butter
thinly.
   —Tea and coffee. Avoid altogether or restrict to 2–3 cups of
weak tea or coffee per day.

   This may seem a spartan diet to anyone used to a regular
intake of 'stodge', but it is largely a matter of realising that our
typical Western diet, relying so much on food that is processed
and de-natured, can be considerably improved by cutting out
the self-indulgent elements. The 'whips' and 'toppings' and
other valueless 'foods' often find a place in our meals only
because we have unconsciously been unable to withstand the
forceful advertising with which they are promoted. Once the
body has been reprogrammed to accept and anticipate whole
food at every meal a return to a 'junk' diet is usually impossible.

So what are the advantages of giving up the habits of a lifetime and changing to a whole food diet? First of all, whole food tastes better. Once you have conditioned your mind to the idea of wholeness it becomes more difficult, as the body shows unmistakeable signs of benefiting, to accept foods that have been processed or 'enhanced' or interfered with in any way. The aim should be to eat foods in as near the condition they were in on being picked or harvested.

Although the whole food message is spreading to the super-market chains some of whom now sell, for example, whole wheat bread, anyone who seriously wants to escape from 'manufactured' food will have to rely for some items on the health or whole food shops. They have acquired an undeserved reputation of being expensive; pound for pound your money is very likely to buy more nutritive value in a whole food shop than in a supermarket.

Does whole food take longer to prepare than conventional food? Most whole food recipes are straightforward and save time rather than increase it. However, chopping and shredding vegetables for the mandatory large mixed salad for the natural diet takes up valuable time at the busiest part of the day for most families because salads should be prepared just before they are eaten. But then think of the time you're saving in not having to cook it.

To Be or Not Be a Vegetarian

Many naturopaths realise that people who have been used to eating meat and fish all their lives usually cannot and will not give it up overnight even if they are told that their health depends upon it. The most realistic advice is to reduce the intake of meat and fish gradually. Try, say, one meatless day per week and on the other days reduce the amount of meat you eat to about 4–6 ozs. Most naturopaths agree that meat should be eaten only once a day. If you can, replace red meat with fish or poultry which contains less harmful fats. Naturopaths also suggest thinking about meat as adding flavour to a predomi-nantly vegetable dish rather than as the main element of a meal. It's a sobering thought that the majority of people in the world are forced to regard meat in this way; others choose to eat meat sparingly and on any objective assessment are healthier for it. It is significant that the long-living people of Ecuador, Georgia and parts of the Middle East are either vegetarians or eat meat only once or twice a week although climatic and environmental factors are also relevant.

Dr E. K. Ledermann of the London Nature Cure Clinic says that in prescribing a meat-free diet it's important that the patient does not feel that following a diet means deprivation. 'I like to help the patient see that it's an exciting project that we're involved in together. I think it's important for the patient to see and understand that this new diet works. After all, the patient attains better health through his own efforts.' Dr Ledermann says that many people are willing to give up eating meat because an interest in nature cure often goes hand in hand with concern for animals. Dr Ledermann also believes that people generally are beginning to realise that eventually our consumption of meat will have to be controlled. Animals reared for human consumption are raised on land which could grow

Any good fruit and vegetable market offers cheap, raw food. However, naturopaths would prefer it to be *organically* grown without the use of chemical fertilizers and sprays.

183

cereals of greater protein value. To produce a pound of meat, a cow or a pig has to eat 20–30 lbs food; even a chicken needs twelve pounds of food to give us one pound of chicken for the table.

Many patients new to nature cure fear that by reducing their intake of meat or becoming vegetarian they will not be getting enough protein. But how much is enough? For much of this century we have been taught that the body must have a considerable amount of protein every day, and that denying the body animal protein is likely to cause illness. This is not true. There have been several studies over the last thirty or forty years which suggest that optimum health can be maintained on about half the amount of protein recommended by Government nutritionists in Britain and America. In Britain the recommended daily allowances of protein range from 65 grams (2.5 ozs) for sedentary men to 93 grams (about 4 ozs) for men with physically demanding jobs; women, active or inactive, should eat 55 grams (2 ozs) of protein every day. American allowances are slightly higher in all categories. Any realistic assessment of the eating habits of most people must conclude that very few regularly attain the recommended allowances of protein. For example, if you have only a light breakfast of toast or a cereal and tea or coffee, a sandwich lunch with beer, tea or coffee, and a meat and two veg meal in the evening you will have consumed only about 50 grams (2 ozs) of protein. You may claim that you are in the pink of condition on such a diet and who is to dispute that? By comparison a well-designed vegetarian regime will contain rather more protein (and vitamins* and minerals) than the typical daily menu.

Even if you are unable to renounce meat and fish altogether many naturopaths will require a new patient, whatever his complaint, to adopt a raw or whole food regime or even a fast for a short period in order to rid the body of the accumulated toxins. Naturopaths believe that all illness derives from the body building up toxins as a result of a poor diet, little or no exercise, and stress. Before the body's restorative work can begin the toxins must be eliminated. Most naturopathic treatment begins with a fast.

* All strict vegetarians are recommended to take a daily supplement of Vitamin B12.

Fasting

Naturopaths ask their patients to regard fasting as a break with the past. During a fast the digestive organs are given what possibly they have never enjoyed – a complete rest from the never-ending job of processing the food that passes from the mouth along the alimentary canal to the bowel.

Although short fasts can be undertaken at home without medical supervision, most fasts of more than three days are normally taken under supervision in residential nature cure clinics. People undergoing medical treatment, or children or older people, should not fast. Naturopaths regard fasting as the most direct method of stimulating the body towards recovery. Animals stop eating, but not drinking, when they are sick. A vestige of this instinct is present in humans who commonly eat sparingly during an attack of flu or a bad cold.

What happens during a fast? Almost everyone who has been to a health farm mentions with pride the heroic achievement of existing for a week or more on water with a slice of lemon added. Most accounts of life on a health farm convey a picture of worn-out, lethargic men and women complaining of headaches, unpleasant tastes in the mouth and nausea, dreaming of fish and chips, gin, beer or doughnuts. This is a true reflection of the fasting experience, but all fasters agree that the first two days are the worst. The body seems rapidly to accept without complaint that its demands will not be satisfied. It is for this reason that therapeutic fasting differs from starvation because the reasonably healthy faster can be sustained for a few days, possibly longer, on the reserves retained naturally in the body. Some fasters of course continue to crave food until the fast ends, but the more common experience is to find that hunger disappears after the first two or three days; this is followed by a 'high' which might last for several days as the detoxification process continues. There is also some satisfaction in the achievement of simply doing without food for a few days knowing that you are cleansing the body.

The first problem most people who want to try a fast have to overcome is how and when to fit it into a busy life. Few can afford to pay £120 plus per week to fast at a health farm. We don't feel ill enough to go to a nature cure clinic for a supervised

185

fast. We don't want to upset commitments or use up valuable holiday time, but we believe that we might benefit from a short period without food. Severe fasts are too demanding and will almost certainly be abandoned, but the following unsupervised fasts (more accurately, semi-fasts) are regularly prescribed for patients at the Bircher-Benner Clinic in Zurich.

Bircher-Benner juice fast

The Clinic recommends that this fast be undertaken while resting in bed for the full mental and physical benefit to be experienced. Other practitioners who recommend one day juice fasts agree that it is possible to carry out light work.

8 am   :   One glass (175 grams – 7 ozs) fruit juice
Noon   :   One glass (175 grams – 7 ozs) vegetable juice (one veg or several)
4 pm   :   One glass (175 grams – 7 ozs) fruit juice
8 pm   :   One glass (175 grams – 7 ozs) carrot or tomato juice

The last two drinks can both be orange juice if preferred. This fast, says the Clinic, should not be continued for more than three days without medical supervision.

Taking the Waters

Water is the most widely used healing substance known to man. In any healing emergency, in the absence of a doctor, we call first for water. Water bathes, soothes, and heals. From the earliest times man has sought out the purest water because instinctively we know that it contains elements and properties which can restore or improve our health. We avoid tainted water because we know it harbours agents that can harm us.

All systems of natural therapy have recommended a regular and plentiful intake of, and frequent bathing in, clean water. The Greeks revered water, regarding it as a magic liquid which contained nearly all that the human body needed to recover or maintain health. They built temples and public baths near

186

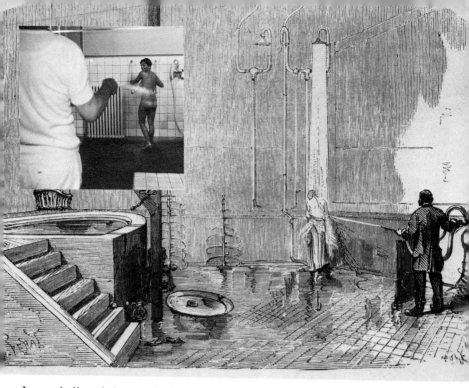

It was believed that as the harshness of the treatment increased, the efficacy of the cold water increased.
Some of today's treatment (inset) remains virtually unchanged, though it has become somewhat gentler.

supplies of natural water, a practice subsequently adopted by the Romans. Their belief in the therapeutic properties of water is continued today in the hundreds of European spas principally in Germany, France, Austria and Italy.

In Germany about six million people 'take the waters' every year. They spend not less than a fortnight at one of the country's 156 spas where they can undergo all the treatments – bathing, massage, sauna, and exercise – which we normally associate with health farms in Britain. Germans take the *Kur* on prescription and most, if not all, of the cost is borne by medical insurance; the aim of German health care is that no one should be denied the *Kur* on the grounds of cost. No doubt some citizens would wish to avoid the *Kur* because in many establishments the regime is rigorous enough to necessitate a further

187

break from work – the *Nachkur* – in order to recover from the weeks of cold baths, enforced exercise and spartan diet. From time to time the usefulness of the *Kur* is questioned, but Germany's usually buoyant economy, presumably produced by a healthy workforce, is invariably cited in justification.

Hydrotherapy or water cure has been a part of European health care since the early nineteenth century when the ideas and practices of Vincenz Priessnitz, an Austrian known as the 'Water Demon of Grafenberg', began to be adopted in other European countries. Priessnitz did not 'invent' nature cure, but developed the ancient practice of applying cold compresses to the body as a cure-all. He is said to have cured himself, after doctors had given him only a short time to live, by applying cold compresses to his chest for a year. Priessnitz had almost total faith in the curative properties of water – not spring or mineral spa water, but plain cold water.

His standard cure for any ailment was to wrap the patient in cold sheets repeating the treatment until the patient recovered. Priessnitz believed that unimpeded blood circulation was essential to health and that all illness derived from what he termed the 'morbidity' of the blood. Most of his patients did recover, and Priessnitz enjoyed considerable fame throughout Europe. His treatments became harsher the more his confidence in the efficacy of cold water increased. Some of his treatments were just this side of torture; for example the falling cold water douche was administered from a bucket or buckets with such force and from such a height that a 'grab bar' had to be provided. In addition to essential water treatment, Priessnitz insisted that good health could only be achieved and maintained through exposure to fresh air, barefoot walking, and regular strenuous exercise. He was not, however, much concerned with his patients' diet.

Priessnitz was responsible for the sitz bath, a common treatment in modern naturopathic clinics. A sitz bath required a patient to immerse himself up to the waist, first in hot water for a few minutes, followed by a similar period in cold water; another version applies the alternating hot and cold water to the feet, a treatment which can be followed at home. Some modern naturopaths recommend a practice, a close relative of the Priessnitz regime, of taking, first a warm shower, followed

188

by a cold shower and then going straight to bed without drying the body. It sounds unpleasant, but in practice it is an invigorating experience; not, however, with a dry partner.

In the second half of the nineteenth century nature cure in Germany was in the hands of Father Sebastian Kneipp of Worshöfen in Bavaria. Father Kneipp was an enthusiastic follower of Priessnitz, but applied his theories with less rigour: where Priessnitz would use a bucket the good Father Kneipp resorted to a watering can. He was as insistent as Priessnitz, however, on early morning barefoot walking in dewy fields or in snow. Modern Kneipp treatment replaces the barefoot promenade with walking in pure water about 12–14″ deep. There are now some fifty spas run on Kneipp principles which are said to benefit heart, vascular, and nervous diseases. Other spas mostly offer specific treatment for rheumatic, respiratory, digestive, gynaecological, gastro-intestinal, genito-urinary, nervous, skin, and childhood diseases. All claim to have a regenerative effect irrespective of specific illness.

British spa treatment, by comparison with the rest of Europe, is non-existent. Enterprising Britons, with a gift for persuasion, can ask their doctors to recommend spa treatment in Europe the cost of which (but not the travel or accommodation) is borne by the National Health Service.

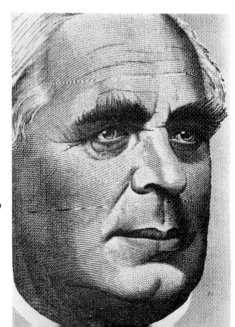

Father Sebastian Kneipp
(1821–1897).

What Is This Thing Called Bread?

It is quite possible that some people born after about 1950 might never have eaten bread; bread, that is, in the sense of a product made from flour, yeast, salt and water. What the majority of people call 'bread' contains all these ingredients, but it cannot and should not be described without qualification as 'bread'. It is a measure of how far our sense of taste has been corrupted that we allow ourselves to be brainwashed into accepting that white sliced bread is tasty and nutritious. That is not to say that white sliced bread has no food value. If it hadn't, our general level of health would be even poorer than it is.

What is it about white bread that so angers naturopaths? They are primarily concerned with the effect that a large intake of white bread and other denatured foods has on children, older people, and low income families. There have been numerous studies which have shown the wasting and degenerative effect white bread has on rats, but most people, even if they knew of these research projects, would not find them particularly persuasive. Rats, after all, are rats.

A more vivid example of the effect white bread has on dental health came in a survey commissioned by the bread industry which found that white bread and jam caused more cavities than white sugar. Masticated in the mouth the bread became

Naturopaths emphasise the importance to health of bread made from unadulterated wholewheat flour.

like flour and water paste which enabled the sugar to get to work on the enamel. Whole meal bread, eaten alone or with sugar, did not turn into glue and therefore did not cause cavities.

Bread is one of the most important items in the average diet. We can hardly avoid eating it at breakfast, and many people consume bread at midday and in the evening. So it is in our interests that it should be of the best quality. In Britain we eat about forty-seven million loaves of white bread a week.

On average we each consume a little over 2 lbs of bread every week, most of it the white, wax-wrapped, sliced variety masquerading under absurd trade names. A grain of wheat is a symbol of goodness, but any significance it might have is lost on the giant bakers of Britain.

By the time it is ready for processing into 'bread' the grain has been stripped of the wheat germ – an excellent source of vitamins B and E – and most of the bran, a major source of dietary fibre. The mineral content has also been severely reduced. To make the flour nutritionally acceptable the law requires the miller to replace only iron, vitamins B1 and B2 and calcium, but not in the quantities originally found in the wheat. All the other nutrients never find their way back into the flour.

The flour is not yet ready for the ovens. It needs additives. No modern food is complete without additives: emulsifiers, whiteners, improvers, stimulators, preservatives, anti-oxidants and bleaching agents; some or all must be present to comfort the corrupted palate. In a typical white loaf there will be about fifteen additives out of over twenty that are permitted.

Naturopaths recommend bread made from 100 per cent wholewheat flour: that is, flour made from the whole grain with nothing added or taken away. They claim that wholewheat bread contains more of all measurable nutrients than the standard white loaf. And it tastes better. You will find wholewheat bread at a good bakery or wholefood shop and at some supermarkets, but make sure that you are buying 100 per cent wholewheat bread. Most bread sold as 'brown' has been dyed; wheatgerm bread is not wholewheat bread. One way of making certain is to bake your own.

Bread making is not difficult and doesn't take up much time. If you're cooking anyway, bread making can easily be fitted in.

191

The Grant Loaf

This loaf was the invention of Doris Grant who was one of the first to warn of, and campaign against, the dangers to health in the processed food industry. She sensibly realised that a complicated, time-consuming recipe was unrealistic and therefore designed one that combined simplicity with economy of time and materials.

> *1·5 kg whole wheat flour*
> *2 pints water*
> *Salt — say 1 or 2 teaspoons*
> *1 teaspoon Barbados sugar or*
> * unblended honey*
> *2 level tablespoons dried yeast*
> *You can use fresh yeast, but dried*
> * works just as well and is far*
> * more convenient.*
> *Optional ingredients include bran*
> * — try putting in about 3 ozs*
> * and increase the water slightly;*
> * experience will tell you how*
> * much extra you need.*
> *Malt makes a moist loaf. A*
> * tablespoon of rye flour has the*
> * effect of making a smoother*
> * textured loaf. A tablet of*
> * vitamin C (50mg or 100mg)*
> * helps the rising process.*

1) Warm the mixing bowl.
2) Dissolve dried yeast in 2 ozs water at blood heat to which sugar has been added.
3) Dissolve salt in water. If you are using malt, add it to the salted water.
4) Place flour in bowl and make a well.
5) When yeast has developed a 'head', stir to make sure it is wholly dissolved and pour into the well followed by the salted water.
6) Mix well. This recipe requires no kneading, but you may find that different flours require more or less water.

7) Divide dough into three greased (butter or oil), floured 2 pt bread tins. Shape with a fork or the back of a spoon, and leave to rise until the dough has reached the top of the tins.
8) If possible place loaves on the top shelf of the oven, but leave enough room for further rising. Cook for 20 minutes at 400 °F or gas mark 6. Turn them around and cook for a further 20 minutes.
9) Remove loaves and leave to cool on a wire rack.

Naturopathy – a New Approach

It is generally agreed that it is unrealistic to expect any change in our attitude to health and illness without the active leadership and co-operation of doctors. There are about 55,000 doctors at work in Britain. It is to them that the majority of people look, and will continue to look, for the treatment of illness. There can be no future for any campaign designed to 'revolutionise' the nature and quality of health that ignores them.

Dr Peter Mansfield is a Lincolnshire general practitioner who is in no doubt that our approach to health, illness, and medicine is in serious need of reform. During his training in London Dr Mansfield began to reject much of what he had been taught; medicine, as he saw it practised, seemed to fulfil neither his nor many of his patients' expectations. His determination to find a workable alternative was confirmed after a meeting with Dr Innes Pearse, co-founder of the Peckham Experiment. This revolutionary project, which flourished just before, and for a few years after, the Second World War in the south-east suburb of London, became a prototype of a community health service that could be introduced into any village, town, or suburb.

The Peckham Experiment was essentially a family club based on premises containing a swimming pool, gymnasium, and meeting rooms. Membership was restricted to whole families who were required to have a full physical examination or 'overhaul' every year and at any significant event in family life, such as a new pregnancy.

Inspired by the Peckham Experiment, Dr Mansfield has established an approach to medicine designed to cultivate

193

'If it hadn't been for all that damn health food, I could have been up here years ago.'

health rather than to treat illness. Dr Mansfield is convinced that poor food is responsible for many illnesses – repeated infections, catarrhal complaints, and degenerative diseases – which we have come to assume are a necessary accompaniment to life in the late twentieth century. All his patients are encouraged to examine their diets and, with his advice, to make improvements. To emphasise the informality of his approach, Dr Mansfield has formed a club, separate from his practice, with aims broadly similar to the Peckham Experiment. 'We are positive,' says Dr Mansfield, 'we talk about health and ways of gaining and keeping it. We ban all talk of doctors, and illnesses past or present.'

Perhaps the most important facility available through the club is the regular health 'overhaul'. Dr Mansfield believes that the comprehensive health check, using all the most sophisticated equipment, gives only a superficial account of the state of a person's health. The object of the 'overhaul' is to help families answer the question, 'How well equipped are we for fulfilling our purpose in life?'

The overhaul is in three stages. First, an interviewer calls on the family at home, to learn about their circumstances, diet, and way of life. Participants are not pressed to discuss private matters. The second stage is a personal medical inspection of each member of the family. They are tested for good physical function rather than structural disorder. Some of the examination techniques are unfamiliar and include a microscope inspection of capillaries in the nail bed and Kirlian photography.* The overhaul is completed by a family conference when Dr Mansfield discusses the findings of the previous stages. 'People enjoy their "overhauls", just as they did in Peckham,' says Dr Mansfield. 'I would like to think that families can build on what they learn from their overhaul so that it becomes part of their daily lives.'

In London there are plans to open a 'Living Centre' run on Peckham Experiment principles in Bermondsey. Advised and supported by Dr James Witchalls, a group of local people plan to convert a disused 'health centre' and reopen it as a place 'devoted to the active creation of health in the local community'. Such an approach may reek of earnest worthiness, but Dr Witchalls and his group see the centre as a place of fun, happiness, and friendship. He believes that any attempt to repeat the Peckham Experiment must be rooted in the informal freedom that characterised the original.

Dr Witchalls, like Dr Mansfield, is a firm supporter of an approach to health, altogether rare today, he says, that depends on doing something to stop a minor complaint becoming serious. On the question of diet Dr Witchalls takes a more pragmatic view. 'It's no good telling a man of sixty that he ought to give up smoking or drinking when it's clear he's well and happy. He'll just laugh and carry on living as he's probably always done. Maybe he's right to do so – as long as he's aware of the risks he's taking. There's more to health than "playing safe" all the time.'

Dr Witchalls believes it's important to regard health as a creative matter. 'Health is a process of growth, of adults and children flourishing in a "nutritious" environment. Given the right conditions, health can be as infectious as disease.'

---

* Kirlian photography is described in 'Healing'.

'Terrible news! An infallible cure for everything has been discovered!'

Useful Books and Addresses

The following list of books will be helpful to anyone wanting to know more about a particular therapy.

All the organisations listed are prepared to offer advice by post or telephone to anyone wanting to consult a qualified practitioner.

General

BRICKLIN M. The Practical Encyclopedia of Natural Healing (Rodale Press, Penn., 1976)
EAGLE R. Alternative Medicine (Futura, 1978)
EAGLE R. Alternative Medicine (BBC, 1980)
HASTINGS A. C. (Editor, with others) Health for the Whole Person (Westview Press, Colorado, 1980)
HILL A. (Editor) A Visual Encyclopedia of Unconventional Medicine (New English Library, 1979)
HULKE M. (Editor) Encyclopedia of Alternative Medicine and Self-Help (Rider, 1978)
INGLIS B. Natural Medicine (Collins, 1979)
STANWAY A. Alternative Medicine (Macdonald & Jane's, 1979)

Institute for Natural Therapies
21 Portland Place
London W1N 3AF

Herbalism

GARLAND S. The Herb & Spice Book (Frances Lincoln/ Weidenfeld & Nicolson, London, 1979)
GRIEVE M. A. A Modern Herbal (Penguin, 1974)
LUST J. B. The Herb Book (Bantam, 1975)
MESSÉGUÉ M. Health Secrets of Plants and Herbs (Collins, 1979)

197

STUART M. (Editor) Encyclopedia of Herbs and Herbalism (Orbis, 1979)
THOMSON W. A. R. (Editor) Healing Plants (Macmillan 1980)

National Institute of Medical Herbalists
65 Frant Road,
Tunbridge Wells, Kent TN2 5LH.
(0892 27439)

The Herb Society,
34 Boscobel Place, London SW1 9PE
(01–235 1530)

Homoeopathy

BLACKIE M. The Patient, Not the Cure (Macdonald & Jane's, 1976)
MITCHELL G. M. Homoeopathy (W. H. Allen, 1975)
SPEIGHT P. Homoeopathy: A Practical Guide to Natural Medicine (Mayflower, 1979)
VITHOULKAS G. Homoeopathy, Medicine of the New Man (Arco, New York, 1979)

British Homoeopathic Association
27a Devonshire Street
London W1N 1RJ
(Tel: 01–935 2163)

Hahnemann Society
Humane Education Centre
Avenue Lodge
Bounds Green Road
London N22 4EU
(Tel: 01–889 1595)

Society of Homoeopaths
59 Norfolk House Road
Streatham
London SW16 1JQ

Osteopathy and Chiropractic

DELVIN D. You and Your Back, How to cope with back pain and how it can be avoided (Pan, 1977)
DINTENFASS J. Chiropractic, A Modern Way to Health (Pyramid, New York, 1977)
INGLIS B. The Book of the Back (Ebury Press, 1978)
STODDARD A. The Back, Relief from Pain (Martin Dunitz, 1979)

British School of Osteopathy
Suffolk Street
London SW1Y 4HG
(Tel: 01–930 9254)

London College of Osteopathy
8–10 Boston Place
London NW1 6ER
(Tel: 01–262 1128)

European College of Osteopathy
104 Tonbridge Road
Maidstone, Kent ME16 8SL
(Tel: 0622 671 558)

British Chiropractors' Association
5 First Avenue,
Chelmsford, Essex CM1 1RX
(Tel: 0245 353078)

Anglo-European College of Chiropractic
1 Cavendish Road,
Bournemouth BH1 1QX
(Tel: 0202 24777)

Hypnotism

BENSON H. The Relaxation Response (Collins, 1976)
CADE C. M. & COXHEAD N. The Awakened Mind (Wildwood House, 1979)
KARLINS M. & ANDREWS L. M. Biofeedback (Abacus, 1975)
LECRON L. M. The Complete Guide of Hypnosis (Harper & Row, New York, 1976)
LINDEMANN H. Relieve Tension the Autogenic Way (Abelard-Schulman, 1973)
MATTHEWS C. Hypnotism for the Millions (Sherbourne Press, L.A., 1968)
O'HARA M. New Hope Through Hypnotherapy (Abacus, 1980)

British Hypnotherapy Association
67 Upper Berkeley Street,
London W1H 7DH
(Tel: 01–723 4443)

British Society of Hypnotherapists
51 Queen Anne Street
London W1M 9FA
(Tel: 01–935 7075)

British Society of Medical and Dental Hypnosis
P.O. Box 6
Ashstead, Surrey KT21 2HT

Centre for Autogenic Training
14a Milford House
7 Queen Anne Street
London W1M 9FD
(Tel: 01–637 1586)

Healing

FRICKER E. G. God is my Witness (Eyre & Spottiswoode, 1979)
MACKINTOSH W. H. The Unwilling Healer (Tom Johanson), (Regency Press, 1979)
MEEK G. W. (Editor) Healers & the Healing Process (Theosophical Publishing House, Illinois, U.S.A., 1977)
TAYLOR J. Science & the Supernatural (Temple Smith, 1980)

National Federation of Spiritual Healers
Old Manor Farm Studio,
Sunbury on Thames, Middx.
(Tel: Sunbury 83164)

Spiritualist Association of Great Britain
33 Belgrave Square,
London SW1X 8QB
(Tel: 01–235 3351)

White Eagle Lodge,
Newlands Rake,
Liss, Hampshire GU33 7HY
(Tel: 073082 3300)

Guild of Spiritualist Healers
99 Bloomfield Road
Gloucester GL1 5BP
(Tel: 0452 25455)

Psychic News
23 Great Queen Street,
London WC2B 5BB
(Tel: 01–405 2914/5)

Radiesthesia and Radionics

BAERLEIN E. & DOWER A. L. G. Healing with Radionics (Thorsons, 1980)
HITCHING F. Pendulum: the Psi Connection (Fontana, 1977)
MERMET A. Principles & Practice of Radiesthesia (Watkins, London, 1975)
RUSSELL E. W. Report on Radionics (Neville Spearman, 1973)
TANSLEY D. V. Radionics and the Subtle Anatomy of Man (Health Science Press, 1972)
TANSLEY D. V. Radionics – Interface with the Ether-Fields (Health Science Press, 1979)
TANSLEY D. V. Dimensions of Radionics (Health Science Press, 1977)
WESTLAKE A. The Pattern of Health (Shambhala, London, 1973)

Radionic Association
16a North Bar
Banbury, Oxon. OX16 6TS
(Tel: 0295 3183)

Psionic Medical Society
34 Beacon Hill Court
Hindhead
Surrey GU26 6PU
(Tel: 042 873 4366)

Acupuncture

A BAREFOOT DOCTOR'S MANUAL (Routledge & Kegan Paul, 1978)
FULDER S. The Root of Being (Hutchinson, 1980)
LEWITH G. T. & N. R. Modern Chinese Acupuncture (Thorsons, 1980)

LEWITH G. T. The Layman's Acupuncture Handbook (Thorsons, 1981)
WORSLEY J. R. Is Acupuncture for You? (Harper & Row, New York, 1973)

British Acupuncture Association & Register
34 Alderney Street
London SW1V 4EU
(Tel: 01–834 1012)

College of Traditional Chinese Acupuncture
Queensway
Leamington Spa
Warwickshire CV31 3LZ
(Tel: 0926 22121)

International College of Oriental Medicine
Green Hedges Lane
East Grinstead
Sussex
(Tel: 0342 28567)

Naturopathy

BENJAMIN H. Everybody's Guide to Nature Cure (Thorsons, 1980)
BIRCHER R. Eating Your Way to Health (Faber & Faber, 1971)
BURKITT D. Don't Forget Fibre in Your Diet (Martin Dunitz, 1979)
DAVIS A. Let's Eat Right to Keep Fit (Allen & Unwin, 1971)
GLASS J. Nature's Way to Health (Mayflower, 1972)
GRANT D. Your Daily Food (Faber & Faber, 1973)
LEDERMANN E. K. Good Health Through Natural Therapy (Pan, 1976)
LEDERMANN E. K. Natural Therapy (Watts, London, 1953)
MANSFIELD P. Common Sense About Health (Available from Templegarth Trust, Templegarth Surgery, Tinkle Street, Grimoldby, Louth, Lincs, price £2 inc. p. & p.)

PEARSE I. H. The Quality of Life (Scottish Academic Press, 1979)
POLUNIN M. The Right Way to Eat (Granada, 1980)
SHEARS C. C. Nutritional Science & Health Education (Nutritional Science Research Institute, 1976)
SHEARS C. C. Orthomolecular Nutrition: The Science of Self-Healing (Nutrition Science Research Institute, 1980)
TULLOH B. Natural Fitness (Arrow, 1976)
WHEATLEY M. A Way of Living as a Means of Survival (Corgi, 1977)

Nutrition Science Research Institute
Mulberry Tree Hall,
Brookthorpe,
Gloucs GL4 0UU
(Tel: 0452 813471)

Vegetarian Society,
53 Marloes Road,
London W8 6LA
(Tel: 01–937 7739)

British College of Naturopathy & Osteopathy
Frazer House,
6 Netherall Gardens,
London NW3 5RR
(Tel: 01–435 7830)

Nature Cure Clinic
15 Oldbury Place
London W1M 3AL
(Tel: 01–935 6213)

Index

205

The Medicine Men

206

207